## Acknowledgement of Country

RMIT students and staff acknowledge that
this anthology was produced and
published on the lands of the Wurundjeri
people of the Kulin nation.
We pay respects to their Ancestors, and to
Elders past and present.
Sovereignty has never been ceded.
We also acknowledge the rich storytelling traditions
of First Nations peoples, which endure and
evolve despite efforts of the continuing colonial
project to silence and erase them.

Always was, always will be, Aboriginal land.

*Prism: an anthology* is published by Clover Press, an imprint of the Associate Degree in Professional Writing and Editing at RMIT University, 23–27 Cardigan St, Carlton 3053, Victoria, Australia.

ISBN: 9780648705635

Typesetter: Shaun Jury

Cover design: Design by Committee

Printing: IngramSpark

 A catalogue record for this book is available from the National Library of Australia

## ABOUT CLOVER PRESS

Clover Press publishes work from the RMIT Professional Writing and Editing programs. The clover, a humble, charming, resilient little plant, spreads far and nourishes many. Its distinctive three-lobed leaves perfectly capture the strength of these programs, integrating the three key areas of writing, editing and publishing.

This name is also inspired by Arthur Clover, a longstanding teacher who retired in 2015. Arthur had two influential mantras: Always Put Students First; and Always, Always, Drink it While it's Fizzy!

The Clover Press logo was created by PWE graduate Ella Dyson.

# Prism

an anthology

# Contents

# Introduction

Penny Johnson

These days I feel undiluted joy when I hold a new book in my hands. I'm delighted that despite the lockdowns and illness, the upending of plans, hopes and dreams, there have been moments where creative endeavour has sparked and flourished. The defiance of the human spirit against the odds. While the dark days seem to have passed, we're still in the aftermath, trying to orientate ourselves, trying to steer our lives back on track or forge a brave new path, trying to work out what the hell we should be doing.

It's in this context that we'll be reading *Prism*, an anthology of poetry, fiction and non-fiction. The theme of this anthology, 'refraction', is given substance here. Instead of the inertia and battening-down-the-hatches of previous years, these stories chart the next stage. They acknowledge the darkness, but seek to shift perspective, to evolve, grow, redirect, burst forth and leave.

I love reading anthologies, which are more than the sum of their parts. The separate pieces jostle against one another, creating connections and juxtapositions that can illuminate and surprise. The volume as a whole assumes an identity for itself, comprising myriad stories, forms, styles and voices.

Readers, you are in for a treat. Some exquisite self-contained stories offer satisfying resolutions: an arm-wrestling match on which much rides, a childless aunt rethinking earlier certainties, a newly single woman discovering more about herself and 'zigazig ah'. Some pieces allow for that delicious pleasure of seeing controlling, unsympathetic characters get their just desserts; others are more open-ended and leave you wondering. And then there are the strange images that imprint themselves on the reader's mind well after the story's end: a splintering glass heart, a spider-infested heart in a teddy bear's chest, levitating grooms in a garden where flowers have gone feral.

Not surprisingly, many settings are post-apocalyptic, where the world is dying or at an end. Humans must fend for themselves, often alone in terrifying circumstances. Other settings are more contemporaneous, where the land has been or will be ravaged by fire and flood, with calamity intensifying the fissures in people's relationships. Fantasy and reality often blur. Darkness too abounds; in the damp soil there is decay and death, as well as a rabbit by the dead tomatoes and a seed tunnelling towards the light.

Relationships are often fragile, and feature loss, struggle and quiet discovery: sons and fathers, sons and mothers, sons and migrant dreams. There are gentle meditations on children, mothers and family. Raw and heart-wrenching is a teenager's numbing account of her first sexual experience. In another story we observe a young married couple unsettled by an interloper.

The authors of these pieces are all nearing the end of their studies in the Associate Degree of Professional Writing and Editing at RMIT. You can tell these stories and poems have been written and crafted with care. Play and experimentation are also on display. The new voices in this collection are assured, resonant and likely to be heard again.

The diligent anthology editing team has played a major part in realising this publication: preparing cover and design briefs, selecting the order of pieces for effect, communicating with authors, and judiciously editing and proofreading. A creative endeavour indeed.

So I congratulate all those involved – the authors, editors and publishing professionals of the future, and their teacher Michaela Skelly – and commend this wonderful anthology to you.

**PENNY JOHNSON** is an IPEd-accredited editor and writes the quarterly grammar quiz for *The Victorian Writer*. She taught in the PWE program at RMIT for nearly twenty years and was program manager from 2013–2020.

# hiraeth;

Ella Pilson

Why not jump in headfirst? What is there to lose? Your dignity? *Please.*

It's water.

It's water, and you've known it your whole life. Just as there was your mother who birthed you, there was the water that held you. The first touch you ever truly knew: water.

There's nothing to fear. It's so vast – it's euphoric. Is it not? The deep blues of distant, far-off nowheres. Something incredible lingering underneath. Think of it as that, as incredible, not something to fear.

You'll never get that far anyway. Look here, where the tide meets the sand. The creamy, white salt froth. What harm could it ever cause you?

If the ocean is so scary, why does it seem to soothe so many? It lulls back and forth, pacifying you in the same hum as your mother's lullaby. Don't you see?

Water was your very first comfort.

And as you grew, you clung to your mother. The way the seaweed hugs your ankles now, tender and warm. It loves you, it all loves you. The sand, piling up over your toes. The sun refracting on the water, shimmering so brightly, a kaleidoscope of blues and greens.

Remember that kaleidoscope you had as a kid? How you peered into it, so intrigued. And yet here you are now, shielding your eyes.

Age has made you cold.

It is age, not the wind, the wind you once greeted so openly. What changed? Where did that dream fade to, that innocence, that desire to treat the ocean like family?

The water would trickle in slowly, tickling your feet as you built sandcastles. So excited to join the moat you dug with grubby fingers. And when you lost your hat. Pink cap on bright waves, teetering on being gone forever. But the water brought it back. And you swore to your mother, you told her that the ocean was alive – your eyes were sparkling then – you told her that the ocean saved your hat. And she smiled, that kind of adult smile that means they know they're smarter than you.

But was she really? Was it really wise to shun this love?

The way you do now, too afraid to do anything other than stand and stare?

It beckons, calling your name. You'll hear it in the shells; you always heard it in the shells. If you were to bend down just once, you'd hear it, faintly. You'd cry. Salty tears gifted by water.

You are water. Your body is made up more of water than of your own mother, yet you refuse to address the ocean by such a name.

**ELLA PILSON** is an author-in-progress based in Naarm (Melbourne). She was shortlisted for the Hachette Australia Prize for Young Writers in 2020 and the YPRL Short Story Competition in 2014. Her works have appeared in the *Eltham High School Anthology* and RMIT's *Catalyst*. You can find her on Twitter @EllaPilson.

# Wildfire

## Cai Bardsley

Cooper leaned against the side of the ute. It was a balmy afternoon and the flies were out. He sipped the last mouthful of warm, foamy beer and tossed the bottle away. It landed in a wilted hydrangea, and two brown hens scuttled out from beneath the bush, one of them returning to inspect the shiny object. *Look at this place*, he thought. *What a dump*. He got in the ute and sounded the horn, a long, irksome toot. On estimation, she would still keep him waiting about fifteen minutes once he got to the horn-beeping stage, so he figured he best get to it. *What is she doing in there?* he thought. Women were a mystery to Cooper. She was probably in front of the mirror, getting all dolled up for attention from some bloke or something equally desperate. He honked the horn again. If she was going to be in there dragging her feet, then he'd be out here beeping his horn.

On the third beep, the flyscreen swung open with force. It smacked against the wall and seemed to flop, as if the life had gone out of it. Marcie could kick the life out of anything Cooper reckoned. She emerged and made her high-heeled way down the steps. Unfortunately for her, she forgot to skip the broken step, and the force of her stomp, combined with the dangerous point of her heel, sent her foot sailing right through it. Cooper began to laugh, a horrible, wheezing laugh. He laughed himself silly, until the sound turned into an evil cough. Marcie looked ready to kill him.

'Fuck you, Cooper,' she said as she made her way over to the ute. 'Wipe that smile off your face, you good-for-nothing drunk. And fix that fucking step.'

Cooper stared straight ahead as he started the car. He artfully deciphered the phrase 'useless as an ashtray on a motorbike' from a string of mutterings as they pulled out of the driveway. Marcie began applying her eye shadow in the small square of mirror on the sun visor, turning her head this way and that.

'Who you all dressed up for anyway?' he asked.

'None of your business,' she said.

'Well, seeing as you're my wife I'd say it is my damn business.'

'Oh, don't Cooper,' she said, rolling her eyes.

Cooper flicked his cigarette out the window and grabbed another from the pack. She hated it when he did that. He rubbed at the ash that had fallen onto his lap, contributing to the large grey stain that had accumulated on his jeans. Marcie's eyes rose to the rear-view mirror and searched the dry grass for a puff of smoke. A fire could nearly start itself at this time of year. The air was as hot and dry as it had ever been, and the roads could melt the tyres off a truck. As they drove on, she imagined flames rising, chasing them along the road, all the way to town. She imagined the flames at home, licking up the driveway, engulfing the house and burning away every remnant of their life. She couldn't decide if it was a nightmare or a daydream.

They pulled up in the car park shared by the pub and chemist, which sat across the road next to the fire station. Large, peeling letters on the front of the pub named it The Wellington Hotel, but everyone just called it 'the Well'. Marcie looked herself over once more and got out of the car without another word.

The pub seemed full to bust and it helped none that the day had been especially hot. Marcie made her way through the crowd, ears ringing with the thrum of conversation, and spotted her book club at a table near the bar. Moving towards them, she carefully avoided Peter McDunn, to save becoming the victim of his conversation. She had no desire to talk of the recent peak in cattle prices or of the chance of fires.

The Tanglewood book club was not so much based around literature as it was around gossip. Amber from the supermarket was in heated discussion with Lianne from the pony club, and the rest of the women looked on intently. Only Jackie appeared to notice Marcie's arrival. Jackie's brown eyes found hers and she smiled, a smile Jackie saved for Marcie. These women thought they could sniff out a scandal, but they couldn't see the one that was right in front of them.

Cooper slammed his fist down on the pokie machine as it swallowed his last five dollars. Greasy Joe cackled wildly on his stool, wobbling dangerously, as his beer slopped over him.

'Shit Coop, you'd be better off trying your luck at bingo with the girls mate,' he said.

Cooper aimed a kick at the leg of Joe's chair, taking it from under him and sending him to the floor.

'Shut your fucken mouth, Joe, before I shut it for you,' he snarled, standing over Joe with his fists clenched.

'Time for a smoke outside, I reckon,' Chippie chimed in as the men began to heckle. He led Cooper out to the car park, where they leaned against the side of his truck. Chip chattered away, and Cooper simmered in silence. Chip was blabbing on about his recent trip across the Nullarbor when he broke off mid-sentence.

'Do you smell that?' he said.

Cooper sniffed the air. His sense of smell was not the best, the result of a lifetime of smoking, but even he could smell it.

'Smoke.'

A sinking feeling had begun in his gut and was spreading through his body like wildfire. His brain had started muttering the unpleasant *what if*. He looked out to the west, where the road led from their house to town, and sure enough there was smoke. Great dark plumes of it, moving towards town.

'Shit,' Cooper said.

It was at that very moment that the alarm sounded next door, and the fire station exploded into chaos.

**CAI BARDSLEY** is a freelance editor and writer working on Wurundjeri land. They are a total grammar nerd and the 2022–2023 student advisor at Editors Victoria. Cai writes fiction and non-fiction in the form of articles, music journalism pieces and book reviews. Find them at caibardsley.com.

# Sir Paul McCartney's Favourite Flowers

### Tess Fletcher

Pinching chips off my plate
     you told me
that you were going to visit
     the grave of Karl Marx
and I thought that was funny
     *Life's a bitch and then you die*
     I told you once
before I learnt
         it was true
Sometimes, in a tight skirt,
         I'm her

The circles under your eyes
     seemed darker, like you,
so, I didn't lean in and kiss them
         Instead, I held three words
     on the tip of my tongue
         for later
Invisible hands reaching for knees

muscle memory
like riding a bike
except that I never learnt to pick myself
back up again

You were drinking a Guinness
and I said
*Like they do in Scotland*
because I always say the wrong thing
when I'm trying to be the right shape
Around you
the world looks upside down
but,
I bet you didn't know
that the flowers of Narcissus
are bisexual

I forgot to ask
about the James Webb Space Telescope
and whether you finally understood
that nothing matters
except The Beatles
Instead, I told everyone
that Biggie Smalls
is much better than Tupac
You said, to impress,
*and then there's Kanye West*
before I smelled jonquils in the air

**TESS FLETCHER** is a creative non-fiction writer, blogger and poet. In the non-fiction realm, her work explores themes of identity, feminism and feelings of millennial melancholy. Her poetry, written under the alter ego @notverypoetic_ is currently preoccupied with love, loss and limerence. She can be found at notverypoetic.com.

# Guilt Trip

### Emily Foundalis

The first hour inside Lincoln's Hilux felt to Paige as though it had the potential to fix everything. Sunshine lit the freeway beyond the dashboard with an unabashed brightness, the breeze reaching through her half-open window to twirl her dark strands of hair together. Lincoln drove, as he always did. And Sienna, Paige's friend of two decades and their ward of sorts for the past six months, stretched herself out across the back seat. She'd been living with them after suddenly needing a place to stay since ending her relationship with her boyfriend. It now seemed to Paige that she was alone in believing Sienna was starting to overstay this arrangement. Regardless, she hoped that dazzling sun and sky could erase her fears.

The car ride from Werribee to Gariwerd would take close to three hours. Every so often, Paige lifted her left hand just past the window and let the sunrays catch on the diamond nestled against her ring finger. If anyone bothered to ask why, she'd say the kaleidoscopic rainbow lightshow flooding the dashboard mesmerised her. But more than anything else, the ring was a reassurance. Whatever rut she and Lincoln had found themselves in of late was temporary; the ring was a testament to his commitment.

Beside her, Lincoln steered with silent efficiency. He kept one hand on the wheel, and the other, his left, rested loosely on the gearstick.

'Where's your ring?' Paige asked him.

'Oh. Yeah. Took it off when I was cleaning the stove earlier.' 'Earlier' referred to the previous evening.

'You didn't put it back on?'

'Forgot. Sorry.'

Paige stared straight ahead at the cattle clustered among the rolling fields. She didn't need to say anything; after eight years together – two of which they'd been married – their displeasure now transcended words. Paige cracked her knuckles methodically, and Lincoln signalled his own ire with his jerky movements on the wheel that lacked the fluid ease of before.

'I'm starving. Can we stop and eat soon?' Sienna piped up.

Paige snorted. 'We ate breakfast an hour ago.'

'Come on. Don't tell me the past six months haven't taught you anything about how much I eat.'

Lincoln laughed. 'Pretty sure there's a Macca's nearby.' He looked into the rear-view mirror. Eyes met and mirth transformed his features. It remained, even when they eventually parked outside the McDonald's. Jealousy troubled Paige like a pebble trapped between the sole of foot and shoe. She indulged in a slam of the Hilux door as she exited.

By the second hour on the road, Paige was unceremoniously demoted to the back seat. It had happened after a toilet break she'd had to campaign for. Somehow, in the time it took for her to relieve herself at the petrol station and return to the Hilux, Sienna had decided she wanted to sit shotgun and play her music in lieu of the radio because the back seat's speakers were broken.

As they'd all hovered outside the Hilux in an apparent stand-off, Sienna had placed a possessive hand on the front passenger door and made her case. 'Please? It's not like there's a seating chart. Leave that shit for your students, Paige. You don't even like the music Linc and I listen to.'

Sienna had hit a nerve. In the rare instances when Lincoln communicated his feelings – usually when he was inebriated – he lamented Paige's tendency to return from work inadvertently treating him the way she treated her sixth graders. 'Emasculating' was the word he'd managed to move his lips around once before moving them back onto his Corona.

Sienna knew. Paige had long ago confided in her about this and other relationship concerns she'd had with Lincoln. Was Sienna poisoning her barbs with the confidences Paige had shared with her?

'But I'm charging my phone up the front.' It sounded undeniably pitiful, but it still seemed preferable to voicing the depths of her desperation: the vain hope that being in the front seat with Lincoln for three hours would be a lifeline. If they could just hold on for these three hours, maybe it'd be proof that they could weather everything else.

'Paige, don't be difficult,' Lincoln said, his tight smile unable to offset his words. Each one landed as if she were merely exposed skin and nerves. 'We already stopped here for you when you could've used the Macca's toilets.'

In the end, she didn't feel she had much of a choice but to agree. Not when Lincoln had relented and taken time off work for this trip only after she'd begged for weeks. She couldn't pinpoint when she'd morphed into the back-pedalling, acquiescent wife fearful of crossing invisible lines. And when she'd bemoaned her grievances to Sienna, her friend had dismissed her concerns because Lincoln never started fights or raised his voice.

Paige wordlessly reached for the doorhandle and climbed into the back seat. As Lincoln pulled back onto the freeway, she dozed off, but not before wondering about husbands who never yelled but never seemed happy with their wives, either.

'Your voice is beautiful.'

'Thank you. That's really sweet of you.' This was the snippet of conversation from the front of the car that roused Paige awake.

'It's the truth. I often think that when I hear you sing around the house.'

Sienna was a horrendous singer. Reminiscent of an off-key Kermit. And maybe it was the fact that Sienna's appetite was endearing to Lincoln but her own bladder was a nuisance, or that he'd so casually banished her to the back seat, or that he and Sienna were now giggling in the front, but Paige had had enough.

'She's as rubbish as you were before your band broke up, and you both know it.'

Sienna's nervous chuckle petered out and Lincoln's eyes found Paige's in the rear-view. A slight shake of his head was all he gave her, yet it was enough to burst whatever bubble he and Sienna had formed. Even if the chasm between husband and wife yawned wider.

Outside, the landscape shifted into the soaring Gariwerd ranges, immovable and enduring against the verdant horizon.

Inside the Hilux, intuition pressed at Paige's gut. It was the type of pressure that warned her they were hurtling towards something irreversible.

**EMILY FOUNDALIS** is an emerging editor with a passion for applying (and sometimes intentionally breaking) grammar rules. When writing, she prefers fantasy and short fiction. She previously worked on issue 211 of *Metro* magazine as an editorial intern. You can find her book review website at emilyfoundalis.com.

# Vena Cava

Claudia Weiskopf

'You're in a bad way! Apparently,
you have developed a soul.'
Yevgeny Zamyatin, *We*, 1924

The heart itches.

Sometimes, when I sleep on it wrong, it hurts. Flips over beneath the warped floorboards of my ribcage, pinches and shudders like a wounded weeping animal begging for the hunter's mercy. Shards slice sideways into my oesophagus, seeking purchase. *Spiteful thing*.

Sometimes it scorches like a radiating sun in the cage of my solar plexus, sending licks of dull fire up the willing ladder of my spine. *Hot, spiteful, bitter little thing*. Heartburn has a new meaning.

But today, it itches. It's the glass dust that does it. When the broken shards rub together, silly kids sharing a bed at a sleepover, crystal sand settles into the hollows of bruised ventricles and leaves them giggling in irritation. I wonder how it would feel to pry out the fragments, wash them under cold water, put them back.

Not easy having a glass heart. Especially when it's broken.

A doctor noticed the first crack at a routine check-up in childhood. Not unusual, he said. Just don't push yourself.

21

Keep inside, keep calm. Bed rest. Nothing to worry about. But the next time he peered into my chest, eyepiece trained on the cold lump living there like a dormant volcano, he frowned. Pulled my parents outside into the hall. I could still hear. The crack is growing. Split off into two, straight into the vena cava. Largest vein in the body.

So it began. Doctor's visits every week. Medicine, meditation, therapy. We must fix the cracks, they said, but the cracks heard and laughed. Grew until the heart was more broken than not; more shattered than shine. So they shrugged. Gave up.

Learn to live with it.

*The hot, spiteful, wicked little thing.*

Not easy having a heart of glass. Not when you're sure that you were made wrong; made upside down and back to front. Not when you're sure that you're from outer space, sent to observe but never touch; to watch but never be watched in return.

Not when the rest of the world has no problem keeping theirs whole. No problem inviting light in so that it might shatter into an infinite array of unknowable colours.

They walk around with their chests shining bright enough to pierce the fabric of their shirts, proud to glow. I wear a scarf to hide the dimness of my own, but still they see. See that I am defective. They all light up blue in sympathy but hold each other tighter, fearful that my broken heart is contagious. But maybe …

I'm on the train when it happens.

It's busy, I'm late and it's hot enough that my shame scarf hangs slick with sweat. The carriage is full of people aflame, hearts refracting snooty rainbows onto the train's faded fabric seats. My shards are clinking pitifully in my chest, dark and dim as always.

I meet the eyes of a child and see her look down at my darkness.

I expect her to turn away. Her chest glows, but softly in the way that only youth does. Her mother sees the child looking, whispers into her ear. Don't stare. But the child does not stop.

Instead, she bends down to her *Peppa Pig* backpack, begins to rummage. Finds what she's looking for. Pulls something out. She leans into me across the chasm of the train aisle and I can see that she's missing her two front teeth.

Can I see?

Her mother starts to speak but I nod. Pull back my scarf. Show her the hurt. The heart shrinks back – unused to the air and trembling like a kicked dog. All hope and fear. She stares at the splinters and under her eyes they are not so horrible. Not so afraid.

Is it painful, she asks.

I nod. The tears are close.

Then, in a hand with glittery chipped pink nail polish, she passes me her gift.

A faded, dirty school-issued glue stick.

**CLAUDIA WEISKOPF** is a Naarm-based author, copywriter, editor and artist. She writes character-driven young adult fiction with themes of magic, queerness, mental health and the natural world. She also contributes non-fiction content to several publications and was a *frankie* Good Stuff awards finalist. Find her at claudiaweiskopf.com or @potplantprincess on Instagram.

# Just Be Prepared for the Smell

### Sarah Maher

I was standing in a cold room – the 'theatre' where they do the surgery. The surgery I needed to witness as a third-year radiography student. It was my first time and the air in the room smelled clean and disinfected: shot through with the pungent stench of diseased flesh. Despite the chill, I was dripping with sweat and one sniff away from heaving. *It'll be fine, it's just like the textbook*, I told myself.

On our way up to the theatre, my supervisor, Jane, had given me the run-down of what I was in for.

'We call it a "lap chole", but its big boring name is laparoscopic cholecystectomy. It's one of the most common procedures we do at this hospital and it's for gallstone disease. They get a laser and just zap out all the gallstones! You'll love it, just be prepared for the smell,' she had explained.

*You're so lucky to get this experience*, I reminded myself.

'Yeah! Sounds good!' was all I managed to get out as we arrived in the gear room. We donned our scrubs, masks, hairnets and lead aprons to protect us from the radiation. There were two aprons left: one had puppies on it and the other was plain black. Jane took the puppies.

'Hey, um, what did you mean exactly by the smell?' I attempted. But it was too late, Jane had already unplugged the portable X-ray machine and had begun rolling it into the theatre.

In the middle of the room, the patient lay unconscious on a slab of stainless steel. They had a hospital gown covering their entire body, apart from their lower stomach. In that area, a team of four nurses had already begun cleaning and shaving.

'Ah, look who decided to grace us with their presence,' the head surgeon, with 'Williams' sewed into his custom lead apron, grumbled from his seat at the head of the operating table as he noticed Jane and me enter.

'Shit, sorry, I wouldn't have brought you up here if I knew he was the head surgeon,' Jane whispered softly to me. 'Good afternoon, Dr Williams. Hey, everyone. Sorry for any inconvenience, we came up as soon as we got the call. I thought Dr Lane was on today?' Jane addressed the group in her calm, professional tone. I hid behind her.

'He took the day off. Can you believe that? I've been saying for years Dr Lane was unreliable and now I'm picking up his shifts!' Dr Williams replied.

'His son got hit by a car this morning,' one of the nurses interjected severely.

'So?'

Awkward silence ensued. The nurses looked at one another with a shake of the head that said 'typical.' The anaesthetist nervously busied herself with her tools, while Jane looked at me and rolled her eyes, whispering, 'Yeah, he's like this.'

Further discussion was interrupted as the surgical site was declared clean and ready to go.

The patient lay still, in the deep sleep of the unconscious. They didn't even twitch as their stomach was incised with a sharp scalpel. I felt the stab as if it were happening to me.

As the team gathered around the patient to plan the procedure, I shied away to the back corner of the room. I stood in such a way that Dr Williams's arm just obstructed my view of the surgical site.

'Are you sure you can see from back there, Sarah?' Jane questioned me.

'Oh yeah. It's actually better because now I can take in the whole room!'

At this point, there was nothing that Dr Williams' arm could have done to spare me from the small fountain of blood that burbled up from the patient's stomach.

'Anyone catch *The bachelor* last night?' The nurses, anaesthetist, Jane and even Dr Williams discussed the show, never missing a beat. Looking back now, I understand all the reasons this conversation may have come about: routine, camaraderie or possibly even blocking out the surgical noises. But back then, all I could do was watch on in horrified awe.

Eventually, it was time for the part of the procedure that required radiography. Jane manned the X-ray machine, screening the patient's stomach so that Dr Williams knew where to focus his attention. At this point, even the black-and-white images caused my stomach to roll.

Suddenly, the clean air was overwhelmed by the smell of rotting, burning meat. At some point, I had been handed laser safety goggles. My vision was tinted dark when I put them on. I directed my attention as far away from the gallstones being zapped by Dr Williams' laser as possible.

I don't even know what happened after that, because at that point, the radiographers were dismissed.

'You handled yourself well in there; there's another one of these tomorrow if you're interested?' Jane asked.

'Thanks so much, Jane. That'd be great.'

As we spoke, I washed my hands, wrists, forearms and elbows. I removed my goggles, hairnet and mask, then put them in the 'dirty' bin. Next to go was the black lead apron. As the six kilograms of lead slipped down my arms and was hung back on its hanger, I found myself standing up straighter than I had in hours.

'I always take a ten-minute tea break after the last theatre case of the day. Wanna join me?' Jane asked.

'Thanks so much, Jane. That'd be great,' I repeated.

Later, in the tearoom, we were drinking coffee and eating Teddy Bear biscuits while scrolling on our phones. I thought of something that I hadn't been able to get off my mind for ages. I googled 'how to start a career in writing and editing'.

**SARAH MAHER** is a lover of words, language and all things bookish. She is currently working as a Melbourne-based copywriter and is constantly in awe of the power of literature. With a keen interest in non-fiction, Sarah's goal is to write material that people can relate to.

# Gladiators

Liam Trickey

'Spit.'

The two boys tore their locked eyes from each other as they each hocked into their right hand a large glob of bubbly spit. Perched shirtless around the tree stump, they knelt in the dirt with rocks digging into their knees. The clearing in the woods was abuzz with the other kids whispering their thoughts on who would be the winner, cracking secret jokes, giggling, shushing.

'Now, take your positions.'

The boys grabbed each other's right hand, their spit squelching together and rolling out the bottom of their firm grip. Some people in the crowd let out cries of disgust and were quickly silenced. The two steadied their elbows on the scratchy stump, all eyes on them as they prepared themselves.

'Remember: there's no shame in losing, but there can only be one winner.'

The warm summer breeze rustled the leaves above. One of the contestants wiped his nose. The other bit his lip. The judge leaned over and cupped both contestants' hands in his. He looked them both in the eyes.

'Ready? Begin.'

The boys sprang into action. The strain was on their faces. Their knuckles were white. The other kids watched, screaming, cheering, shouting insults and encouragement. The hands began to fall one way and a roar spread through the crowd, but the struggling wrestler pulled back through gritted teeth to stabilise. Their faces grew red and their arms shook from the struggle. The judge circled the entangled battlers with a smirk, his eyes fixed on their quaking fists. The crowd jeered, voices broke, people howled and the circle pit pulled in closer.

'Give it to him!'

'Come on, come on!'

'Let's go, muscles!'

The fighters were still locked in a dead heat. They both had one hand at war, the other gripping the stump for dear life. The splinters in their hands and the rocks under their knees be damned. They only thought of victory. The judge leaned in close to one boy.

'You think you can hold it? Looks like it hurts.'

The boy tried to ignore him, wincing from the strain. The judge held his face close for another second before turning to the other boy.

'He's looking like he's got you beat. Just admit you lost. Let go.'

The second boy opened his eyes to glare at the judge before growling. The crowd pulled in even closer as the tension built.

The judge stepped back. The boys' brows began to sweat. One shifted his knee in the dirt and opened his eyes. His small red face lit up as he fixated on the battling knuckles. He drew all his strength and began to twist his wrist. The other boy shifted as well, but looked worried. The crowd drew in even further, sensing an ending. The boys shouted, screamed, howled. The crowd grew feverous. The judge moved in, preparing to make his judgement.

The fists fell, one red and strained knuckle knocking against the wood of the stump. It was over.

The crowd cheered and grabbed for their champion, who felt a strange mix of elation and complete and utter exhaustion. He fell backwards into the dirt, wheezing. The other boy turned away and fell onto all fours, breathless and with tears beginning to well in his eyes.

As the crowd celebrated, the judge moved through them and grabbed the loser, picking him up by the arm. He knelt and brought an arm around him, then took him by the waist and brought him over to the winner. He stood up and the two sweaty, panting boys locked eyes. The loser wiped snot from his nose. The winner just smiled. They slammed into each other in a deep embrace, no longer children, but champions, both.

**LIAM TRICKEY** is a freelance copywriter and storyteller. By day, he helps brands that give back to the community, and by night he writes fiction that discusses the big questions. He currently works with Market Lane's marketing team, bringing sustainable practices to your daily coffee. Contact him at liamtrickey1@gmail.com.

# Left Behind

### Nicole Priest

I broke up with my boyfriend on a Tuesday, before lunch.
That morning, I woke up to find death confronting me. Last night the possum had been fine. But now, he was most certainly dead. My last survivor.

I stared at his little body, transfixed by its stillness.

I'd always known I'd outlive him. But reality was something different. I didn't count on feeling so alone and without purpose.

I buried the possum next to the others: my little circle of failure.

On the tombstone, a cereal box, I wrote 'The Last One'. It chilled me to think that I probably wouldn't get a grave when the time came. My parents never did.

I stood outside for a long time. If I retreated into the house, that would have made it real.

This was exactly what Marcus wanted. And for that I could never forgive him.

The house was really an old shed on an isolated farm north of Melbourne, abandoned during the early days of the devastation. We had been here for almost three months, along with a few other refugees from the city. And the possums.

△ △ △

I had been drawn to the wildlife sanctuary in the days after. Most of the animals had remained. People were dying in the street, so saving threatened species was not foremost on everyone's minds. Someone thought to open the enclosures, so kangaroos spilled out onto the road, creating more havoc for anyone trying to escape the city.

All I saw were the fractured remnants of the Leadbeater's possum enclosure.

These were the last of a critically endangered species. They were survivors, once thought to be extinct before miraculously reappearing late in the 1960s. They had spent the next sixty years battling against the logging industry for precious tree hollows, before their numbers dwindled once more.

And now I'd ushered in another extinction.

Marcus thought I was the worst for bringing them with us. But this was how I survived – by concentrating on the survival of others.

I had studied conservation biology at university, but a thesis on olive ridley turtle distribution wasn't much to recommend me for all our survival.

When anyone thought to ask, I said I was a biologist. An 'observer of life'. The irony. I had only just graduated when the world fell apart.

Homo sapiens no longer populated every corner of Earth.

I couldn't save them either.

'A freaking possum, Bree! Get a grip.'

Marcus didn't understand. We had met while everything was imploding, and if you had to survive in a post-apocalyptic wasteland with anyone, he was probably your best bet.

'And we could've eaten them. For God's sake.'

It would have been like consuming my own flesh.

Most would agree that it was commonplace not to put animals before other people.

But this was how they survived – by prioritising their own survival over every other species.

When I was six, Dad took me to see the thylacine exhibition at the museum.

'What happened to them?' I asked.

'They hunted them.'

'Didn't somebody want to protect them?'

'They tried. But it was too late.'

I decided then that I had to fight to save the endangered world.

I had no idea that one of the next endangered species would be humans, merely one century after the extinction of the thylacine.

In early 2030, the situation was already dire, but we didn't yet realise the full extent of it. There were restrictions on everything from petrol to milk, and daily carbon emissions were being monitored. Mum said it was a precaution. 'We should put a plan in place, just in case.'

A solid plan, but it never quite worked.

Millions of people were displaced once the rising seas submerged their homes, and the worst-hit areas experienced mass migration.

Getting into Australia, as per usual, was never easy. But desperate people tried.

There were still plenty of nonbelievers. They held protests outside Parliament House claiming the government was restricting their freedom.

Our neighbour, Mrs Bronson, was one of them. She used to put signs on her front lawn among the garden gnomes and hydrangeas.

She died in the first week.

I don't know what happened to the gnomes. I guess they were left behind.

△ △ △

My grandmother had dragged me to church a few times a year and tried to convince me to join the youth group. I was never a youth-group sort of person. Or a religious sort of person.

My grandmother's house, shrouded in rainforest, would probably still be standing. Dad used to kick the stone foundations. 'This old bugger will survive a nuclear war.'

△ △ △

Marcus and I lived very different lives, and if it wasn't for all of this, I doubted we would have got together at all. He would have picked someone smart and beautiful and self-assured, to match his own endlessly bright eyes and cursive stare, if only I hadn't sought refuge in his barn among the dairy cows the day of the firestorm. He was presented with a pixie of a girl, splattered with mud to match her hair.

The looming end of the world tended to influence one's choices.

Three months later, here we were.

But I didn't want to be the Eve of a doomed generation.

△ △ △

Our break-up went well. 'Marcus, I just think that … we're not meant to be, you know? Our relationship seems purely circumstantial.'

'Are you saying we should see other people? Because I don't see many other people here, do you?'

Mum always said that if you can't imagine yourself with someone at the end of the world, you shouldn't be with them at all.

(She never said that, but she should have.)

'Bree, are you crazy? You can't leave. You'll be dead in days.'

'Maybe I am already.'

△ △ △

I left no trace of existence behind. I would be as extant as the possums and the thylacine.

'This old bugger will survive a nuclear war.'

That was where I'd go.

---

**NICOLE PRIEST** is a writer and customer service officer. She has worked as an online content writer and a book-group officer at the Centre for Adult Education (CAE). Nicole writes fiction and non-fiction about the environment, and is currently working on her first novel. Find her work at nicolepriest.com.au.

# clicks

Ky Nolan

*click click click*
the click of my bic lighter is titillating
as it promises
a cancerous moment of mindfulness

for the benefit of my mind

                                        at the cost of my lungs

everything in          equal balance

                                  one organ for another

cool concrete grounds me soundly to the lawns of the State Library
observing the careening verse of commuters streaming past like a
silent film, I wonder

do strangers ever observe me?

*scratch scratch scratch*
my pen busily scrapes its way over the page
recording my
                    thoughts
                            for the day

an impermanent record
for this page will eventually perish
swallowed up by the never-sated appetite of deep time or crumpled
and smashed until it is ash which may someday float on a distant
breeze and return to the boundless sky

I scratch the thoughts down anyway

a lively toddler squeals with glee as her mother races to catch her and

some seagulls cackle as one of their comrades
                         shits
                          on
                  Charles La Trobe's head

a melody of clicks and scratches measure the minutes that escape
me as the afternoon
   *d i s s o  l   v   e   s*                        into early twilight

*click click click* – not my lighter

              pen resting softly at the base of my chin
I'm pulled from my reverie
reminded that the purpose of my perching here was to be mindful

looking up, I discover the source of this unfamiliar sound

a few feet away,
a tourist stands and peers at me through a multifocal lens

there is no-one else around and
the camera is pointed                                    right at me

                    [ I am centre frame ]

momentarily dazzled and suddenly self-conscious I struggle to
return to my prior
                                        distracted state

movements now affected from strained concentration
I try to imagine how I must have looked, in order to replicate it:

I see

                    a lover of literature
peacefully seated at the foot of their mentor:
a neoclassical monument to the written word
pen furiously scribbling under auburn skies
while the day dies
eyes ablaze with delight
and staring  t h r o u g h  the page and  i n t o  their unencumbered
imagination

thank you, tourist
you caused me to pause and look back at myself and

for a moment

one fleeting, flickering moment

what I saw was marvellous

---

**KY NOLAN** is a writer, editor and cameleer based in Naarm. They collect words, and love attending spoken word poetry nights. They're currently working with the Small Press Network (SPN) as an Associate Producer for the 2022 Independent Publishing Conference. To hire a camel, find them on Twitter @kynolan_.

# Vision

A.I. Bartolo

M y vision trembles.
The pinkening sky shakes and cracks.

The shards of sky rumble against one another violently, like tectonic plates.

Their fault lines twist like deformed arms, reaching out to each other, but struggling to keep hold under the pressure. Something stirs within me.

The shards give way, taking the grass and clouds and sky with them as they fall, like a shattered stained-glass window.

A new image takes their place.

I hear 'Derek' being called for, but we're the only two in the room.

'Yes?' I hear myself ask.

'You were saying?'

'I' – my head aches and spins – 'was?'

I'm propped up on a brown leather couch. The rug beneath it is white and square against the dark mahogany floor. Across from me is a man in a grey armchair that matches the roots of his thick and otherwise-brown hair and beard. He could look jovial, but his deeply furrowed brow kept that from him. He's tapping a pen against a clipboard.

'About the room, Derek,' he clarifies in his grizzly voice. 'What's in the room?'

I look at him wide-eyed for a moment.

'Couch. Rug. Bookshelves. Desk. Window. Chair. You.'

'Really?'

I raise an eyebrow.

'What about what you were saying before?'

I think for a moment and it's like my brain melts, but in a nice way.

'I saw . . . a pink sky, darkening into a deep purple the further up you look from the horizon. The sky was starless, but the moon was so big. And white.'

I close my eyes, trying to find myself in that place again.

'The grass I sat on was a deep green, the kind of green that grass isn't. I could see the wind twirling in the air like ribbon. I could feel an animal by my side. A dog.'

The man gives a lifeless chuckle.

'Take a look at your side.'

I open my eyes. Brown boots are on the ground.

'Those aren't a dog, are they, Son?'

'No. They're not.'

He drags his ballpoint pen against his clipboard, and the sound echoes in my ears.

The echo turns into a panting turns into a shout turns into a shriek. I cup my hands around my ears and clench my teeth. My eyelids are shut so tightly that the black is deepened by louder blacks. My whole body tenses.

'Derek.' I can barely hear behind the sound. 'Listen to me. Focus on my voice. Think about where you are.'

I see skies. Pink ones and blue ones and green ones and brown ones. The grass is all kinds of green: chartreuse, moss, olive, emerald and brown. All kinds of dogs bark at me, baring their teeth. I'm shrieking over them.

'Couch. Rug. Bookshelves.'

My brain spins, vomits into my skull and drips down my spine.

'Desk. Window. Chair.'

The dogs quieten, and the shrieking in my throat softens. I slowly drop my hands from my head and stretch my legs back out.

'You.'

I open my eyes, and the man is still sitting in his chair, his legs crossed. The noise stops. He gives a soulful smile.

'Welcome back.'

I look through him. 'What is this?'

'This is a psychologist's office. I am Dr H, but you call me Henry. We are good friends, Derek.'

'Derek?'

'That is your name. You are twenty-four years old. You work just down the road from here. In finance.'

Henry's words echo in my head, cementing themselves in harmony. 'But what about back there?'

'There is no "back there", Derek. That place isn't real.' There is a brief pause, and time freezes for a moment.

'It felt real.'

'Derek,' Henry repeats. 'Think about right now. What can you physically feel, in this very moment?'

I can feel the leather of the couch on my arms as I lean against it, and the armrest supporting my neck. My shirt – the brown one I wear to the office – rests on my shoulders, and the sides of my head are comparably colder than the top. There's a bit of a crick in my neck.

'Doesn't that calm you down, Son?'

It does.

'Remember this feeling. I want you to do this exercise every day for me, okay?'

I nod.

'Good. Now, I'll see you next week. Let me know how tonight goes.'

'Tonight?' I search my brain for any sort of connection, but all I know is this feeling.

'Yes, with your date,' Henry says with a smile. 'You're going to the Italian restaurant across the street from your apartment and meeting Allison Sheleigh Prim there at 5 pm. Your good friend and work colleague, Jack Orson Dells, introduced you to her three nights ago. It was at the museum – remember, you really love the museum. Your date would have been sooner if it weren't for the overtime your boss so often asks of you. You're going to wear a nice lilac shirt and clean black slacks, but you'll bring your brown jacket in case it gets cold. You have a good feeling about this one.'

'I do.'

'That's what I like to hear, Son.'

Henry walks me out of his office and into the brown hallway. He gives me a pat on the back, a smile and bids me farewell. I walk home to my apartment, which is across the street from the Italian restaurant. I put on my nice lilac shirt, clean black slacks, and make sure to bring my brown jacket in case it gets cold. I meet with Allison Sheleigh Prim at 5 pm and we have dinner. I feel good about it all. Once the bill is settled, we step outside, and it has gotten cold, so I put on my jacket. Allison gives me a kiss on the cheek, steps into a car and drives away. I cross the street, get back into my apartment and lie on my bed, still dressed. I curse my boss for all the overtime he has given me and the overtime he will undoubtedly give me again. I stare up at the grey ceiling.

**A.I. BARTOLO** is a fiction editor and young-adult fiction writer with a flair for the dramatic. They spend their time writing hard, reading harder, and perhaps playing hardest. You can contact them at aisaiahbartolo@gmail.com.

# Never Say Never

## Linda Chen

B rett leans over and says, 'Let's go. I've had enough of these rug rats.'

I cringe and look around. Thankfully, the adults nearby are busy running after their children or talking a mile a minute. Watching the parents, including my younger brother and sister, something stirs inside me. 'They haven't had the cake yet,' I reply.

'Oh, that's another half-hour gone.'

'It's chocklit cake!' says my three-year-old niece. She's on my lap as usual, playing with my hair. A gentle warmth comes over me. When the cake with candles appears, she makes a beeline for it.

'I thought you wanted to drop into that winery on the way home.'

'We'll still have time. It doesn't worry me if we don't make it today anyway.'

'You, passing up the chance to have a vino? In eight years, that'd be a first.' Brett smirks.

I roll my eyes. I'm thirty-five now, and together we've done some amazing trips to Europe, Asia and the US. Brett keeps talking about our next big trip, to Africa, but for the first time I'm not excited about it. I don't want to be away from my family and friends for so long.

Brett can't have children. He doesn't want them either. That suited me perfectly – I thought. They're too much trouble, we agreed. There were so many other things we wanted to do with our lives.

'It's not easy having children,' my mother said, time and again. 'I could've had the time of my life if I didn't have you three.' I often wondered why she did have us. At fifteen, I made up my mind that I would never have children.

As soon as the cake is finished, Brett says, 'Come on, let's go or we'll miss the winery.' My niece runs up to me, chocolate cream around her lips.

'Aunty Hannah, when can I come to your house?'

I lift her up and cuddle her. Her hair feels like silk. I stroke her smooth, soft cheek and give it a kiss. 'Very soon,' I say, smiling. Aware of Brett's glance, I look away. My face feels flushed.

I grab my handbag and push the IVF pamphlet down, firmly out of sight. Now's not the right time. Brett will remind me; we had an agreement.

**LINDA CHEN** is an emerging writer who enjoys writing short stories, children's stories and non-fiction. She believes in the power of connecting people and communities through sharing personal experiences and stories. Linda values writing that is culturally inclusive, providing different perspectives and voices.

# Things My Cat Is Teaching Me

Clara Johanna

### Lesson 1: don't apologise for enjoying your own company

Cats exist comfortably in solitude. When they want to be alone, they feel no desire to justify it. They don't care about labels like introvert and antisocial and INFP and Pisces moon.

When my cat wants my company, she seeks it. There's no resentful *will I won't I should I* about going to the party or the dinner or the coffee catch-up, only to go, and end up waiting – jaw clenched – until it's acceptable to slink off, tail between her legs.

Cats are independent until they're not – until they're tripping you up on your bleary-eyed 7 am stumble down the hall, fusing to your legs and screaming *pet me/feed me/scratchbehindmyears/ love me love me love me*.

When my cat wants to sit on my lap, she'll sit on my lap; claim it her throne. Me, her loyal subject. When she grows bored of me, I'm her object. The clumsy thing who fumbles around the house and mutters to itself at weird hours, sleeps through its alarms and forgets to take its meds but never, ever forgets to feed her *or else*.

I'm learning to say *thank you* to my cat when she sits on my lap and *thank you* again when she leaves, and to save my rejection-sensitive dysphoria for someone who cares.

**Lesson 2: sleep when you can and nap when you want to**

Cats sleep an average of twelve to sixteen hours a day as a way to preserve energy for *the hunt*. I'm lucky to force five, and I spend the remaining clumsy and noisy – the antithesis of stealth.

Cats *carpe diem*. More accurately, they *carpe crepusculum*; revel in those low-light hours of the in-between, where streetlights and sundown mingle in neon and pastel.

In the midafternoon, my cat sidles over and circles my lap twice anticlockwise, before settling her chin against my knee and sleeping the daylight away.

I've taken to joining her on my days off, lying on the floor with my limbs askew, chasing patches of sunlight on the hardwood.

Hours later when I'm boiling the kettle and considering a camomile, she claws the walls with cocaine eyes. In bed, my restless legs make easy prey.

Sleep has always felt slippery. My 2021 *Spotify Wrapped* was metalcore and boy bands and 2,527 hours of white noise. This year's might be different because now I have her purring, that soft contented buzz, the antidote to my dystopian dyspnoea. Between bouts of shadow-chasing, she curls into the crook of my elbow and settles my nervous system into sleep.

**Lesson 3: only speak if you have something to say**

In their first weeks of life, a cat's meow is reserved solely for its mother, to express hunger or discomfort. In adulthood, cats no longer need to communicate like this. They reserve their meows for us – their looming, blundering, mostly bald guardians – bombarding us with tiny soprano bullets, those same feline instincts of hunger and fear and the all-consuming desire for attention *nownownownownow*.

I make noise all the time—

to fill silence, to apologise too much for things that aren't my fault and not enough for things that are, to cry when I should be happy and laugh when I'm overwhelmed, to project every single festering insecurity and doubt and desire onto the person sleeping next to me, constantly confusing comfortable with co-dependent.

My cat sits and watches birds out the window for hours on end. Listens to me mumbling and ranting and crying and laughing and talking tedious, meaningless, incessant shit. She gives no response because it does not warrant one.

I need to stop being the girl who cried wolf and start crying cat instead.

## Lesson 4 is one for both of us: sometimes weakness can save you

Cats are skilled at hiding their pain. Deeply entrenched predatory instincts have taught them that displaying weakness is certain to put a target on their back. You'll find sick cats hunched under beds or behind couches or in bushes where they've crawled to die.

I feel the same most days – lashing out with chalkboard claws and words even harsher, or dragging myself mute under the covers – anything before admitting that maybe-probably-definitely *I'm not okay.*

I once read that for a cat to lounge stretched out, belly exposed, is reassurance of their complete trust in you. On my bad days, I lie with my body curved fetal, spine like a question mark, none of my delicate parts on show.

My cat is teaching me about sleep and solitude and soliloquy, but there are some things she does not know. Some of her instincts I must reject. I need to learn the difference between delusions of dignity and a certain death wish; that is to say, there isn't one.

So, when my cat grows old, her bones brittle and instincts sluggish, I will hold her close and say, *I see you.* Let's stalk shadows at midnight and sleep sprawled in the afternoon light, our fragile underbellies on show.

**CLARA JOHANNA** is an English as a second language (ESL) teacher, English tutor, and staunch Oxford comma advocate. She lives on Wurundjeri land. When she's not dissecting similes and syntax with her students, she's slinging lattes at her local and figuring out how to subvert the writer-barista stereotype. You can find her existential poetry and experimental memoir at clarajohannaborg.com.

# Unexpected Saviours

Leann Rose Dumas

This is an excerpt from a larger
work, 'Blame It on the Rain'.

'What, this – no – this can't be right. I *studied* for this for a whole *week*.'

Anna's voice strains, looking down at the C that precedes her name on her chemistry test. Although she's captain of the gymnastics team, she isn't an idiot. Despite what all those stupid little drama shows depict.

'I'm sorry Miss Winter, but your results don't match what you're saying. There were questions that you should have known the answers to, given your outstanding track record. They were all small mistakes, but they added up to something bigger,' Mr Daniels explains steadily.

The room seems hazy. Never in her life has she ever received anything below an A. All through high school she's been getting A+'s and now here she is, standing in the middle of an empty classroom, her chemistry teacher looking at her with one of those stupid apologetic smiles, and a large red C staring back at her. Taunting her.

Her eyes sting and her chest feels tight. The amount of baggage she's accumulated in the span of half a day is excruciating. In a split second she's running out of the classroom, the sound of her footsteps heavy in the bare hallways.

She races out through the front doors of the school and is hit by the late afternoon air. The hugging coolness fails to comfort her as she rushes down the concrete school steps. She chokes back her sobs while she runs through the car park.

Why does everything have to be so hard for her? Why can't she just live a life with no expectations to be great? *Why? Why? Why?*

It's only when she reaches her car that she realises she's left her purse with her car keys in it inside her locker. It seems the world has decided that it's 'Fuck Anna Winter Day'. She groans and sinks down onto the asphalt, hugging her knees tightly under her chin. She finally lets out one hearty sob. Perfection has never felt so painful.

What is her mother going to say when she finds out? God, her mother's going to find out. She hangs her head. She can't seem to control her breathing as she imagines that look.

Before she can continue her mental breakdown, a shadow falls over her. When she looks up, her heart clenches. The last thing she wants is the all-star footballer of Park High School witnessing her downfall.

'C'mon. I want to take you somewhere.' Lily's voice is soft.

'Aren't you supposed to be in class?' Anna rubs her face in an attempt to gain composure. It's kind of embarrassing really, Lily seeing her like this. It's like being caught unzipping a costume. A costume Anna has worn her whole life, afraid to let anyone get a glimpse of who she really is.

'I have a free,' Lily answers quietly. Of course. It seems Lily May always finds a way to not be in class. Something Anna can never bring herself to do.

Lily holds her hand out. Anna stares at it for a moment.

'I'm not gonna bite. C'mon,' Lily says with a gentle laugh, shaking her hand.

Deciding that she really doesn't have enough energy to stay sitting here all glum, Anna puts her hand in Lily's. The warmth is comforting, but Anna pushes her heels into the ground when Lily starts to lead her across the car park.

'What's the matter?' asks Lily.

'Where are we going?'

And all Lily needs to do is smile that charming smile.

'Just trust me.'

The three words that pass through Lily's lips are so delicate and warm. Anna just nods, letting Lily pull her towards her car.

△ △ △

They've been driving for fifteen minutes now, Anna silently looking out at the scenery. It's sort of weird how not weird being in silence with Lily is.

'You don't have to do this for me.' Anna speaks up through the quiet, tearing her eyes away from the window to turn and look at the girl behind the steering wheel.

'I think I kind of do,' Lily replies tenderly, the corners of her lips twitching up to form a smile.

'Why?' Anna shakes her head, still unable to believe that Lily has really picked her up from the middle of a breakdown. 'After me being such a total and utter bitch to you, why would you even want to help me?'

There's a silence.

They reach a red light, the car slowing down to a stop. Lily turns to look at her, dark eyes locking into light ones.

'Friends help each other out, right?'

*Right ... Friends ...*

'Yeah,' Anna nods, her eyes moving back to the road. 'Yeah, they do.' If Lily and Anna can find things in common, there's hope in everything.

Anna doesn't know why her chest feels tight. *Friends.* That's what she told Lily they should be. *Just. Friends.*

**LEANN ROSE DUMAS** is a Filipino writer based in Melbourne who specialises in LGBTQIA+ romantic fiction and poetry. In 2020 she self-published a poetry book, *Yours Sincerely*, which can be found at leannrosedumas.com. She can also be found on Instagram @leannrosedumas and @leannwrites.

# Time

## Samantha Whitehouse

This is an excerpt from a larger work, 'Up in Flames'.

Time fractures into the *before* and the *after*, and I float through the week following the bushfire in a cloud of pain relief, restlessness and trauma. I've had two surgeries on my hands: one to remove any dead skin and clean whatever is left, and another to take skin from my thighs to patch my palms and fingers. I have very little movement and feeling in them now, but the burns were only – I laughed when they said 'only' – second-degree, which means I should see some improvement over time.

My stay in the intensive care unit lasted a few days, and I was moved to the burns unit when my lungs cleared. Claire was moved to the surgical short stay unit yesterday, and Piper only stayed one night before being allowed to go home. I'm trying really hard not to resent her for that.

We're sitting in the *after* on the Saturday following the bushfire. Well, Mum and Tyler are. When the clock hits three – the same time, I later found out, that we were trying to escape – I'm sitting in the bleak, dizzying moment of *during*.

'I need to see Claire,' I say, completely interrupting Mum and Tyler's conversation. They're sitting on either side of my bed; Mum always on the left, Tyler always on the right. They might do that on purpose. Mum goes home overnight to check on Dad, but Tyler is allowed to stay, and in the early hours of the morning, when the nightmares hit, it's my right arm that jerks out first. We haven't spoken about it, but Tyler catches me every time.

'We'll have to ask if you can go over, Sweet,' Mum says, making no effort to move. Tyler notices this to, and frowns.

'They're allowed visitors,' he replies, rising from the chair.

'How do you know that?' I ask.

'Piper's been a few times.'

'Oh.' I don't ask how he knows this, or why she hasn't visited me. Last Saturday might be a blur in parts, but I do remember our screaming at each other.

Mum's voice cracks as she speaks. 'Well, she can't just walk over there.'

'I'll get her a wheelchair, it's okay.' Tyler squeezes Mum's shoulder then slips out of the room, the door clicking shut behind him.

Mum sits back in her chair, defeated.

'It's okay, Mum.' I say, sliding off the bed to stand. Mum cringes, but I don't wobble or use the bedhead for support like I did a few days ago. My knees have small patches on them to keep the blisters healing properly, and the tops of both my thighs are bandaged, covering the stitches they used to sew me back up after the grafts, but neither give me as much grief as they did before. There's an orange tinge to the tape holding the bandages on my hands in place, I notice as I stare at them, trying to find words. I'm safe. I'm okay.

I thought I'd be annoyed at having to be wheeled around in a chair, but I'm so tired from crying that I don't care. Tyler helps me from the bed to the chair, then he takes me across the hospital to the short stay unit, Mum quietly walking behind us. When we reach the ward, we head for the nurses' desk. Tyler and Mum start fidgeting while we wait for someone to help us, but my gaze catches on someone sitting in the waiting room. They're wearing all black, with green-rimmed glasses sitting on the bridge of their nose. I go to wheel myself over there until I realise I can't. I know I should ask for help, but I don't want Piper to see. So, I get up, a little unsteady, and I walk over to where Piper sits, taking the seat beside her.

'Hi.'

'Hi,' she says without looking up from her hands folded in front of her, 'how are you?'

'Fine,' I answer, a clear lie, 'you?'

'Fine.' Also a lie.

'Tyler said you'd been here a few times.'

'Yeah.' I watch as Piper takes off her glasses, rubs one of her eyes, her black nail polish chipped. 'I, um …' she coughs to clear her throat. 'I didn't think you'd want to see me.'

'Yeah, well … it's not like we left on good terms.'

'I guess not.'

'You know I didn't mean it, right?'

'I know. I didn't either.'

'Mm.' I try looking her in the eyes but she's still staring at her hands. Tears have welled in her eyes. I clear my throat. 'Look, I wouldn't have actually left you behind.'

'But you did.' Tears mix with Piper's words. She sits back and rubs her hands over her face. She looks like she hasn't slept all week. 'You left me,' she says with a breath.

'To get Claire,' I say, finishing her sentence. 'I had to go back for her.'

'You left me,' she shoots back, shaking her head, 'you didn't even look back, you just ... you ran.'

'Are you seriously upset about that?'

'Wouldn't you be?'

I sink back into the chair, dumbfounded. I watch her but she doesn't turn to me at all. 'Would I be upset if you'd left me – someone very capable of following a track out of the bush – to run back and help your friend who was pinned by a burning log as a bushfire raced towards them? No, I wouldn't.'

There's a beat's silence, then Piper puts her glasses on and stands up. 'Then that's the difference between us.' She looks at me now. There are no tears in her eyes, just a stoic expression. My heart is pounding. 'You only care about what serves you and no-one else.'

Piper turns on her heel and walks away, back past the nurses' desk, where my brother smiles at her, down the hallway and into the elevator, leaving me to sit with her words.

---

**SAMANTHA WHITEHOUSE** is a lover, writer and reader of young adult fiction. Her favourite books to read and write are ones that make you cry or throw them across the room. Find her @sjwhi_ on Instagram for reading rants and photos of her dogs.

# Bright Stones

Mitzi Swan

My children move through me,
and into this world they come,
gazing into my face
the look they give is not a hunger,
like a cat intent on a bird,
but a conduit, and a taking in

ah, I am human they cry,
and for at least that moment
they know they belong

they focus on this me they see
it's no small thing
I will bend them this way or that,
show them an imperfect spectrum
there are always some colours
that will cut and bleed

later the world will become their medium,
bend them this way and that

black can turn to green
and green can turn to black

I sit on the front step,
worn boards warm in the sun
my baby tugs at my breast
this house faces a tower, a hoop pine,
spiked green-black all the way up to the blue,
and in the distance a small mountain,
its familiar curves shaping a somehow comforting mystery
the mountain ties the earth to the sky

I pass through these days in a confoundment of detail,
square white nappies pegged on a wire,
the smell of a browning apple core
my baby crawls along with a plastic three-legged lion in her teeth
my toddler carries around a button in a box for a day,
shaking it every now and then
my son sees a rollerskate in an op shop and looks to my daughter
'Shoe on wheels,' he says, nodding gravely

My children bring me stones bright with water and they turn
from my face to the world.

---

**MITZI SWAN** is an editor and writer of non-fiction, fiction and poetry. She loves photography and film and the way that words and pictures can wrap together. She is currently working on a collection of essays, poetry and images, a combination of memoir and reflection. Find her at mitzi377.wixsite.com/mitziswan or @mitzibird on Instagram.

# Alice

## Sam Reed

Alice got off the tram and waited for the lights to change, staring across the road at Federation Square. Trust Michael to want to meet here, he'd love it, with all its trendy eateries serving pretentious, overpriced cocktails. He should have known she hated that sort of thing, but he probably didn't. After fifteen years of marriage, she didn't feel he knew her at all. Though maybe her hating it was the point. They were getting together on the advice of their lawyers, a friendly lunch so they could discuss the custody of their children.

While they were married, Michael hadn't lifted a finger when it came to parenting, and now he was pushing for equal custody. As a professor of ethics he probably felt he had to. You couldn't give lectures on morals to impressionable young women and also be a layabout dad. Hell, maybe she should let him have joint custody. See how he likes it. But she couldn't do that to Eric and Julian. They wouldn't want to live with him.

The lights changed and Alice joined the crowd as it surged across Swanston Street. Stepping onto the footpath, she peered across the square searching for Onnand's, a BBQ place she'd booked. Michael had wanted to go to a vegetarian restaurant, but she'd put her foot down. She'd spent fifteen years not eating meat for Michael and was looking forward to watching him search through the menu to find what scarce morsels Onnand's had to offer vegetarians.

She saw the restaurant across the square and started towards it. In front of the glass facade a scruffy young man with a backpack gesticulated wildly. His t-shirt bore the slogan MEAT IS MURDER. 'Animals have feelings too,' he yelled. 'Rich inner lives cut short by your barbarity.' He tried to block Alice's way. 'What right do you have to take their lives for your pleasure?' Fuck. She was heading for a lunch where she'd have to deal with Michael's self-righteousness, she didn't have time for this. 'Think of the chickens, shivering on the conveyer belt . . .' She reached up and shoved him right where his shirt said MURDER. He stepped back, startled. Alice pushed past him and entered the restaurant just as he found his voice again. 'You'll regret it. There'll be retribution . . .' The door closed behind her.

The lighting was dim, the restaurant noisy with diners. Alice spied Michael, his head buried in the menu. She walked over and he looked up. 'Really?' he said, his voice thick with the question. Christ, who in their forties said 'really' and laced it with that much sarcasm? Michael wasn't only screwing twenty-somethings, he thought he was one.

Alice sat down. 'Really, what?'

Michael glanced around the restaurant. 'You thought this was a good idea?'

'It's my kind of place.' She picked up a menu and scanned the dishes. What to get for the most impact? Prawns? Ten little deaths to make one meal. Would that piss him off more than a steak? Was a crustacean's life worth less than a cow's? Alice didn't know, she hadn't studied ethics.

A waiter emerged from the darkness to take their order.

'There's literally nothing here I can eat,' Michael said.

'How about a Caesar salad?' Alice smiled at him.

'That's got bacon in it.'

'A Caesar salad, hold the bacon.'

'That's just a salad.' Michael closed his menu. 'No food for me, but I think I need a drink. A gin and tonic.'

'Make sure it's not Beefeaters,' Alice said.

'Please, Alice. We're trying to be civil.'

She ignored him, decided that surf and turf covered all bases, and ordered it. The waiter made a note and left them alone.

'Okay, the way this is going, let's make it quick.' Michael crossed his arms over his chest.

'You're not getting joint custody.'

'I'm not going for joint custody,' Michael said, and Alice relaxed for the first time all day. Maybe she should go easier on him; but then she remembered the twenty-somethings.

'I'm thinking you get the kids every second weekend.'

'They're thirteen and fourteen.' Michael uncrossed his arms, softened his posture. 'They're old enough to have some say in who they live with.'

Alice cocked her head and smiled at him. 'And you think they'll choose you?' She was astounded. Was Michael that divorced from reality?

'On the weekend, after the movie, I sat them down and asked them. Carefully. I didn't want to influence their decision.' Of course he didn't. The fucking ethicist again, always fair, always balanced. He was a nightmare to live with, never just doing something, always pondering the rights and wrongs. How could anyone want to live like that? Certainly the boys wouldn't. But then something nagged at her. If they didn't, why was Michael mentioning it?

'And?' she asked, her voice wavering.

Michael looked at her with pity in his eyes. 'They want to live with me.'

'Live with you?' She spat the words at him, his pity fuelling her fury. 'What, while you fuck girls scarcely older than them in the next room?'

'For God's sake, it was one affair, and it's over.'

'There's no way they'd choose you over me. What have you ever done for them?'

Michael sighed. 'Look, Alice, it's not like you're a lot of fun to be around anymore.'

'Me? Not fun? I'm . . . I'm . . . gre . . .' Alice couldn't get the words out. She pushed her chair back, stormed to the exit, shoved open the door and bumped into the protestor coming in, his backpack hitting her in the side. She was twenty paces from the restaurant before she wondered why a vegetarian protester would be going into a BBQ restaurant. As she turned back she heard a faint cry of 'Meat is murder!' and the restaurant's facade exploded in a flash of glass and smoke. The blast forced Alice back a few steps and ash rained down on her. The smoke started to dissipate, revealing a burnt-out shell where the restaurant had been. 'Well, Michael,' she muttered as she wiped the ash from her face, 'you're not getting custody now.'

---

**SAM REED** is a writer, director and animator. He has produced award-winning animations for a range of clients – including MTV, the ABC and Unilever – in Australia, Vietnam and the United States. He is currently working on a noir crime novel, 'Stockdale'. To view his animation work, visit samreedfilm.com.

# St Peter's Vineyard

## 911

### Yvonne Sanders

The old man stood silent in the cool of the early spring morning. He stepped forward, peering through the breaking light. The ground underfoot was dark and wet. Too dark and too wet. The vines, fully laden and heavily bowed the night before, now seemed taller and straighter. He extended his curious hand, tenderly searching for the full-bellied grapes, their promise of a rich harvest at last arrived.

△ △ △

Rózsa understood the new world augured a more fortunate existence than any post-war Hungary could hope to offer. Yet the bitter blade of longing slashed at her. She ached for her parents and sister, left behind in her beloved homeland. The cost seemed unendurable. For Jozsef the cost of remaining held the same truth. The truth was they barely survived the German occupation. The Soviet occupation that followed proved crushing. Any semblance of freedom once enjoyed was long lost, so too any hope of its return. Then came the autumn of 1956, with its disastrous harvest, inflaming an already devastated economy. Fuel shortages, low wages and unemployment paved the way for domestic unrest.

The uprising was inevitable for a proud people holding tight to the nebulous memory of sovereign rule – an uprising countered by the formidable invaders intent on extinguishing the rising tide of national consciousness.

By then, Rózsa was already with child. For Jozsef there was little work – not enough to feed the pair, let alone the impending needs of the child that was coming. Then came the letter, conscripting him to fight the Soviet cause against his own people. This he could not do. The time had come to execute his ominous plan, one he had prayed fervently never to need. Yet it had come to this. He could not leave Rózsa. He could not abandon his new family. He could not continue to fail in his provision. He would not demean himself to the treachery of Soviet enlistment.

Jozsef instructed Rózsa to dress warmly – several layers, with coat and scarf and hood. They prepared rations. But there would be no luggage. No goodbyes to family and friends. No packing belongings and sending them on. There could be no outward sign when dawn broke of anything different from the night before, save their absence.

Rózsa yielded to Jozsef's instructions. Tentatively. She knew not of his plan. He had confided in no-one. Not even her. In the deep of the night, when all was still and pitch, they gathered what little they could hide inside their garments, then stepping outside, pulled the door closed behind them. Vedo looked up from his station by the cottage door, attentive and curious. The old dog rose, clinging to Jozsef as he moved along the path. Jozsef dropped to the ground, embracing the dreadlocked Komondor, his loyal companion. He whispered into the dog's ear. Vedo sat obediently and did not move. Jozsef stroked the hound one long last time, then turned away. 'Come,' he said, taking Rózsa's hand and guiding her on. Rózsa began to understand. She turned, looking back at their home and the sorrowful whimpering of the dog that did not move. She swallowed hard, wiping away the tears.

Then she turned back, toward an unknown destiny.

Jozsef and Rózsa endured excruciating days and nights amongst menacing forest shadows, trudging by night, silent and still by day. Then sweet relief as they crossed the border and into Austria. Safety.

Vexing bureaucracy and a tumultuous voyage later, they reached Australia. Their son was born.

Peter Stephen.

Born an Australian citizen in the dank medical quarters of the Bonegilla migrant camp.

They had planted a new life in this strange land with this tiny child.

They settled where the work took them, in far north-western Victoria – prime grape-growing country. Jozsef toiled long and hard, nurturing the vines, reaping the harvest and stocking the cellars for an esteemed and prosperous vineyard.

Peter was a bright, curious child who thrived in the new country. A studious, ambitious boy, he excelled at all his endeavours. While it pained Rózsa and Jozsef, they encouraged him to study in the city, where his passion for architecture could better be pursued. They swelled with pride when he graduated. Steeled themselves when he accepted a prestigious assignment interstate. Their melancholy turned to heartache when he secured an impressive posting that would catapult him even further away. New York City. The World Trade Centre.

Every day Rózsa prayed for her son. Every day she missed him. Jozsef did not pray. Instead, he tended his own small vineyard in the far corner of their garden. St Peter's Vineyard, he'd called it, in honour of his son and the saint for whom he was named. Now in his retirement, it was one of few things that brought him joy. It was September and his first harvest. The grapes were full and round and ready. He would give them one more day.

Tomorrow, the harvest.

Jozsef rose early, as was his habit. Rózsa too was up, preparing their morning staple of plum jam on sourdough and a jug of brewed coffee. Jozsef could not wait for the breakfast ritual before stepping outside to behold his crop. Pulling on his boots and coat, he strode out into the crisp air.

The telephone reverberated its shrill warning, shattering the morning's tranquillity. Rózsa listened in numbing horror. She fell heavily against the wall, lifting her apron to catch the tears. She stumbled to the door, pushed against it.

'Jozsef,' she bleated.

The old man stood silent in the cool of the early spring morning. He stepped forward, peering through the breaking light. The ground underfoot was dark and wet. Too dark and too wet. The vines, fully laden and heavily bowed the night before, now seemed taller and straighter. He extended his curious hand, tenderly searching for the full-bellied grapes, their promise of a rich harvest at last arrived.

Their empty skins hung long and lank in Jozsef's hand. He fell to his knees, sinking into the mud, bloodied by the crimson elixir.

*Dedicated to my husband Paul Stephen Gyulavary, and to his twin brother Peter Mark Gyulavary who we lost in the terrorist attacks on New York City on 11 September 2001.*

**YVONNE SANDERS** is a Melbourne/Naarm-based writer of long-form fiction, short stories and flash fiction. She has been published in *The Victorian Writer*, and short-listed in the Lord Mayor's Creative Writing Award and the Sisters in Crime Scarlet Stiletto Awards. Yvonne is also a science writer, nature lover, bushwalker and birdwatcher.

# On Family

## Kristin Brodie

You are standing tall and proud. Your hand lightly resting on a parasol; just a whisper of a touch. Your dress is long, elegant and stately; high-necked and with a matching hat that is perched on the top of your head. I see your eyes, how they are slightly turned down at the outer corner, and in them I see my sister, my dad, my aunties. The photo is black and white, but I know exactly what shade those puppy-dog eyes are; they are the same blue that I have seen all my life.

The planes of your slim face and your straight nose and your rosebud lips are intimately familiar to me. They are Brodie features. I have the Brodie name, but I do not have those features. I have the Evans features from my mum's side of the family. How funny that you're full to the brim of Brodie features, but you were never a Brodie. You were a Blood. Granny Blood. And probably something else before that.

Shakespeare asked, 'What's in a name?'[1], and it is clear when I see this photo that family is made up of so much more than just a name. Family is something that you are wearing on your face and in the way that you are holding yourself. It is quirks and traits and habits and tradition too.

The Brodies I know are stoic, loyal and Catholic. Brodies are roast lunches on Christmas Day, and Grandma's special ice cream. They are people of few emotional words but with plenty of small talk. They make things and they fix things. They tinker. They take things apart and put them back together again, just to understand how they work. Brodies value quality, artisanry and skill. They are craftspeople. Brodies look after their possessions and have them for a lifetime.

I wonder how much of this comes from you, Granny Blood. Were you a tinkerer, like the other Brodies I know? I hope so. Perhaps there are different kinds of tinkerers, and maybe I do my tinkering with words. I create and play with and take apart words, like my dad does with wood and my grandpa did with machines.

Brodies are fiercely independent and you, Granny Blood, seem to have been no different. They say you chopped your own firewood until the day you died. I wonder how many of your traits are within me, and how many of my traits come from others within my lineage that I will pass down the family line.

I found this photo of you at my grandpa's house, after he died. The family went over to look through his house and sort through the stuff which made up his life. We walked through the house and picked up everything we saw, and it felt invasive and rude and bizarre all at once. It is hard to piece together a person based on the objects they left behind. Were we assigning undue value to things we perceive as valuable, but which were actually junk to Grandpa? Were we unknowingly tossing aside the things that were the most special to him?

My dad and his brother, Paul, sorted through all of Grandpa's tools and all the projects he had going on in his shed. Paul went back home to Western Australia after the funeral. He could take with him only what would fit in his suitcase, so most of Grandpa's possessions are with my dad. Of all Grandpa's possessions, I gravitated most to this photo of you. However, my dad and Paul had eyes only for your blue screwdriver.

The blue screwdriver. It was Grandpa's favourite. Neither Dad nor Paul could quite articulate what made this screwdriver so special, but it featured heavily in their childhoods. No matter how few tools Grandpa could take somewhere, the blue screwdriver always made the cut. There was plenty of playful arguing about who would get it now. The elder? The younger? The brother with the fewest screwdrivers? Wherever it went, I'm sure Dad polished it up to restore it to its former glory, before it found its new home.

Brodies know the value of things and the importance of taking care of them, so my dad is building a chest for the tools from Grandpa's house that are going to his brother. It is a coffin-load of tools. An heirloom-in-progress. On its lock, Dad is going to engrave three sets of initials. His own, RB; his brother's, PB; and his nephew's, JB. Jack Brodie is my cheeky little cousin, but JB is also James Brodie, my grandpa.

I wonder how many of the Brodie traits you carried, Granny Blood. I do not know much about you, other than your name and the story of how you died. Our family lore says that you lived to be 107, and that one day, while you were hanging out your washing, the wind knocked you over and you died.

I imagine you like the last leaf hanging onto a tree in autumn. The Brodies are a skinny bunch, so at 107 you would've been tiny. In my head, you're hanging onto a sheet or a large pair of knickers and hanging on for dear life while the wind fills them up like a sail to take you away.

What a way to go and what a thing to be famous for. If it weren't for such a story, you might have faded out of our family's mythology. You're wearing a serious expression in your photo, but I wonder if you would find the humour in your story as much as everyone who hears it does.

As you stood for your portrait, it's unlikely that you imagined that one of your descendants – your great-great-granddaughter – would find it and treasure it. That she would feel like she knew you even though the worlds you inhibit are so different.

[1] William Shakespeare, *Romeo and Juliet* (1597)

**KRISTIN BRODIE** is a reader, writer, editor, and Oxford comma enthusiast living and working on Wurundjeri land. She has worked as a marketer, copywriter, freelancer, an English tutor, and in corporate communications. When she isn't reading or hanging out with her dog, she's tending to her out-of-control collection of indoor plants. Find her at kristinbrodie.com.

# Zigazig ah

## Marion Taffe

I come home from work and he is gone, at last. I kick off my shoes and feel the cool floorboards beneath my feet. I walk through my little cottage, feeling the quiet space embrace me. It's not that we fought. Fighting might have been *something*. Instead, we nothinged. The nothing took up so much space in the house, in my head. It was big, dark and heavy. Now it is over.

△ △ △

Saturday morning, I sit in a cafe and order a latte. I take the book I've just bought out of its brown paper bag. I run my fingertip over the gold ampersand, which weaves through the *a* in War and the *a* in Peace. I fold back the cover. A crease. A beginning.

'*Eh bien, mon* prince, so Genoa and Lucca are now merely estates, the private estates of the Buonaparte family …'[1]

It reminds me of Paulo, a lovely Genovan I met on a train in Italy years ago. He'd taught himself English by memorising Spice Girls lyrics.

'What is this "zigazig ah"?' he'd asked. 'I looked in all the English books. I listened to all the English songs. I asked all the English speakers I met, but they laughed at me.'

'It's made up. It doesn't mean anything,' I said.

'It means nothing?' Paulo said. 'So, they were singing, "I really really really wanna – nothing"?'[2]

'Maybe zigazig ah sounded better than nothing?'

He laughed and I laughed. We laughed at the nonsensicality of it all with the beautiful Ligurian countryside rolling past our window.

I order another coffee. I try to grasp the Russian empress, the prince, the lady-in-waiting and the long, unfolding line-up of characters. Try to pull them from the tiny print. Try to make them real. Try to care. Three coffees later, my head hurts, my heart flutters and I can't remember what I've just read. I put the book away and walk home.

I fill my spare time with nothing much. Cooking, watching television, throwing out undies with holes in them. Sometimes I look at the book, at that snaking ampersand, but I don't read it.

A few Saturdays later, I eat breakfast in my backyard, which is lawn, a stump and a clothes line. I need a garden, I decide. A few herbs. A few veg. A few green metaphors for a new start. The stump is the perfect spot. I've never paid it much attention. It was there when we moved in. It is charcoal black in patches, probably from a failed attempt to burn it out. I take a shovel from the shed and start digging, but the stump's roots are all through the soil.

At the hardware store, I tell the man I need to dig out a stump. He says I need muscle to dig out a stump. 'I have muscle,' I say. He smirks, sells me a mattock. A pick at one end and a flat scraping thing at the other.

It is warm. I strip down to a tank top and shorts. I put on boots, gardening gloves and a hat. I spread my feet and lift the mattock, two-handed, over one shoulder. I inhale and swing the pick hard into the earth. It slips in deep, cracking through the roots. I lever the handle again and again, delighting in the sounds of snapping wood and the dirt on my lips, the grit in my teeth.

My hands slip and I need to feel my grip, so I lose the gloves. I dig a ditch around the stump and smile at the pain of a purple blister on my soft office hands. I sweat and grunt and swing the mattock as hard as I can. I dig out the Russians, the lost years, the lost hope and the happily ever after. I cry, I sing, I wipe my nose on the back of my hand. I dance to Spice Girls songs.

The stump seems sad now, half its roots cut off from the earth, encircled by a boot-printed ditch. I imagine the tree as it might have been. Growing from a seed. It would have sent white roots down. Hair thin at first, fattening and spreading. Did children climb in its branches? Did lovers kiss in its shade? Did it grow fruit? Acorns? Gumnuts? I can't tell.

I grip the mattock again. This time I stand on the stump and swing the mattock under it, working my way around. Until finally, I give the flat head of the mattock one more swing. I leave it there, hooked beneath the stump. I take a deep breath and pull on the handle. I growl and close my eyes. Muscles burn, roots snap. The handle gives faster, faster. Then, with a great long grunt that comes from an unknown place within me, the stump comes up.

I let it thud back down. I drop the mattock and collapse, star-fished, onto the dirty lawn. The grass prickles my skin and the sun turns my eyelids red. I use the last of my strength to get up and haul the stump out of the hole. I stand, looking at the empty ditch. It's a big hole, but it's not nothing.

The next day is Sunday. I plant the garden, wash my hands and put *War & Peace* on the bookshelf. I send a silent thought to Paulo, wherever he is in the world.

I finally understand zigazig ah.

---

[1] Leo Tolstoy, *War and Peace* (1869)
[2] Spice Girls, 'Wannabe' (1996)

**MARION TAFFE** worked in newspapers for twenty years before leaving to have children and dance with words. Her work-in-progress is a historical novel that draws on themes of rage and creativity. Marion was awarded a 2023 Varuna Fellowship and was runner-up in the 2022 Grace Marion Wilson Emerging Writers Competition.

# Last Ditch Effort

## Blaise Katherine

The car rocks from side to side, kind of like a creaky ship navigating a choppy ocean swell, but instead of rolling waves, the vehicle struggles to overcome the muddy ruts and holes that litter the ground beneath its wheels.

I grip the seat in front of me firmly, stomach continuing to churn. I've put all my trust in Jess so far, so why should that change now? I watch with widened eyes as she locks the steering wheel to the left, and soon I feel nothing but the sliding of the tyres along the slick wet ground outside. An hour ago, I'd been so sure that she would be able to get us through the bush, but things are taking all the wrong turns.

'Well, shit.'

Jess tries to wrench the wheel back over before it's too late, but the car's movements are beginning to feel suspiciously rigid. My heart sits heavily in my throat as the vehicle jolts, a metallic groan erupting from its weary frame as it finally gives up the fight. It shudders to a standstill, and I hear Jess revving the engine a few more times before she sighs. 'Nope, we're bogged.'

My face falls and the two of us exchange a look through the rear-view mirror. If we're stuck *this* far from camp with the storm due to hit at any moment, there's no hope for us. I can see how Jess slumps in the front seat of the car, shoulders sagging low.

The silence is long and uncomfortable. I glance at the darkening clouds outside, fighting the urge to start biting at my nails. 'It's alright. Let's just get out and see how far in we are.'

So that's exactly what we do, not that it makes the situation *better* in any sense. We soon realise that the car is essentially beached. Bottomed out in the ditch with nowhere to go and nobody going with it.

'Happy New Year, I guess?' Jess follows her words with a half-hearted chuckle, trying to lift the mood. I groan loudly and fix her with a pointed look.

'What if it's a sign? Like ... we're all doomed to fail our exams this year or something.'

'Bro, don't even say that.'

With no phone service, all we can do is crawl back into the car and wait for help to cross our path. The bags of ice sitting in the boot are probably nothing but packaged water at this point, though I can't find it in myself to check.

'There's the rain.' Jess' voice pulls me out of my thoughts. I glance over to see her reaching her hand out of the open window to feel for the droplets. I have to force myself to take a deep breath, feeling my hands start to tremble. Storms are just not my thing.

'I have an idea,' Jess says suddenly. Her tone is serious and her blue-green eyes feel like they're boring into my own. 'What if we ... just use the rain to our advantage?'

'Huh?'

'Think about it.' She sits up in her seat. 'The rain makes the ground all slippery, and then we put this baby into neutral and push her out!'

'Your wording is so gross.'

'Who *cares*? What have we got to lose here?' she pleads. I feel myself caving under her stare, but the niggling doubts won't leave my head.

'The mud will make it impossible,' I reason, even though I know she's right. It's not like I have a better plan to offer. Jess rolls her eyes, opening her car door and stepping out into the rainfall that's growing heavier by the minute.

'That's why we do it at the right moment. Come on!'

A loud yell of frustration bubbles up in my chest, but I swing my own door open before Jess can say anything else. She's right; this is literally one of the only things we can do right now. The wind is beginning to pick up through the small trees around us, the incessant rustling of their brittle leaves setting my nerves alight once more.

'Okay, it's now or never!' Jess shouts above the racket.

I follow her lead, feeling the muddy ground beneath my feet start to give way as we heave against the front of the car. It feels like how I imagine trying to roll a granite boulder up a gradual slope would – pointless and painful. That's until the car suddenly lurches backwards, taking us along with it in a crescendo of screams.

'It moved!'

We pick ourselves up from the mud, ambitions running on a newfound fuel. Soon enough, the car starts rolling further backwards, escaping the clutches of the ditch in a combination of momentum and mobility.

'No way,' I say, voice raspy with exhaustion and hair flecked with mud. 'We actually got it out!'

'Damn right we did. Let's go. Quick!' Jess's shout snaps me out of my thoughts.

I swiftly follow her back to the car, clambering inside to be greeted by the sound of ragged breathing and shoes in the sorriest state I think I've ever seen. I look over at Jess and she looks back, the two of us breaking into laughter not a moment later.

'I'm never letting you drive again.'

**BLAISE KATHERINE** is an editing enthusiast ready to divulge knowledge on strange, albeit intriguing, subjects. When writing, she specialises in romance and young adult fiction, all while aspiring to become a fully-fledged editor. Ideally, she'll be working with a diverse range of authors after graduating. Contact her at blaisekatherine.editing@gmail.com.

# Red

## Olivia Byrne

Red has always been my least favourite colour
and I don't think it'd match my room decor.

Red as bloodshot eyes staring at a computer screen
desperately hoping for some inch of anything.
Red notification, red heart, and
God, I love the colour red.

Although I'm not really sure if it's the colour red I like.
Imagine splattering it on the walls and just rubbing your
hands in it,
you could tell any story about yourself that you like.
I wanna do that but there's no paint, there's no nothing.

So, you've decided to decorate a little bit.
But there's no red notification, red heart or red pyjamas.
You've already pulled the trigger and you've fucked it
because it doesn't match your room decor and wow,

Mum is gonna hate this mess you've made.
It's just like her papa's.
God, I hate the colour red.

**OLIVIA BYRNE** is a freelance writer and social media manager. She is currently working with some of the biggest fashion companies in the world to create online content.

# Rot

## Ruby Hilton

The ultimate destruction of his arbitrary life boiled down to the corpses knocking on his car window. Tommy was slow waking up and greeting them – slower than someone living at the end of the world should be. He tugged his thin blanket over his shoulder, curling further away from the door, shivering with the morning frost that leaked through from outside. His knee throbbed from the armrest digging into it all night.

'Nick,' he grunted. He'd been shoved up into the front by Nick last night, so the least he could do was stop the corpses from scratching up the glass. One of the dead bastards groaned, like it was some great inconvenience that Tommy wasn't offering himself up for breakfast – but no-one ate breakfast anymore. It was way better to save food for night-time, with the dying embers of a campfire and a quiet song strummed on a broken guitar. When there was nothing to distract from the gnawing starvation that gripped inside. The type of hunger that made you realise the corpses weren't that separated from their original form.

One of them thumped their limp hands against the window, agitated.

'Nick,' he grunted again, this time huffing and turning his face against the red crushed velvet to peek at the rear seat.

No-one was there. The car was empty. Tommy squinted and rubbed sleep from his eyes with the heels of his palms. He pressed them into his sockets and dragged them along his skin. Nick wasn't there, because Nick had gone to fill up their waterskins before dawn, because Nick barely slept and hated sitting around in silence. It was now a good hour or two past sunrise, and Nick hadn't come back yet, because he would never let so many dead ones surround the car. They were there because Nick was gone.

'I fucking hate you,' Tommy said to the invisible Nick. He spun back around and slammed his skull against the headrest and gripped the steering wheel in front of him. The keys were in the ignition, ready to turn at a second's notice. For a moment, Tommy entertained the thought of leaving Nick in the dust; watching him curse Tommy and his childish ways in the rearview mirror. He and his audience laughed; rather, they hissed at the noise, but Nick wasn't there to appreciate his humour so he pretended they were laughing.

Tommy reached over to the passenger seat and fumbled through the pile of clothes and empty packets of out-of-date crisps for his knife – a rusting kitchen knife they found when they were scavenging through a restaurant a few months ago – and rolled open his window just enough to fit the blade through. It took a few minutes of awkward stabbing until the group lay still on the ground, poking at their heads until their brains were too screwed up to function. And then the door wouldn't open because they were all squished against it, so he had to climb to the backseat and escape from there.

'Jesus,' he huffed. Tommy marched across the asphalt road, through the itchy, dry grass and into the tree line. There was a small clearing with a swift running stream, a hollow log and the remnants of last night's campfire. There was no Nick.

There was no blood either, or tattered clothes or bones ripped from a body. No dropped shovel, which was Nick's weapon of choice. He carefully searched around, jumped over the stream and looked up in the trees and kicked at dead leaves until he was sure there was nothing he had missed. Tommy sat in the dirt. He poked at the ash of their campfire, traced around a footprint that pointed to Nick being here not that long ago.

He wiped his hands on his pants and stood. 'Nick!' He shouted. Screaming out in the open was never a great idea these days, but Tommy was getting annoyed. He searched the area again. When Nick went on his dumb walks, he always left a path to follow. Normally he tied scraps of fabric – collected from all the places they'd stayed – to fences and signs. So, either Tommy was missing them, or Nick hadn't left them out. And if Nick hadn't left them out, then he was in trouble.

Tommy searched again. He climbed up a dying oak and squinted through the leaves and across the road. Nothing. The world was quiet. There was a gentle breeze that grazed his hair, cooled his face, that definitely wasn't getting flushed and hot the way it usually did when he was flustered. In fact, the wind was cold enough to excuse his shaky hands when he cupped his mouth and shouted out Nick's name again. He hadn't put on his jacket.

From the south, there was a storm brewing: grey clouds getting heavier and darker and closer. They'd be here soon, with the wind strengthening and bringing them over. He'd been afraid of storms for years, and in the open, by himself, the distant roll of thunder trembled down his spine like the plucked string of a guitar. He sat, leaning against the dusty car. A drop of rain slid down his forehead. He would wait, he decided, until Nick returned. He would wait until the metal rusted and the asphalt cracked and his body rotted into the earth. He felt like moss was already growing in his lungs, making every breath soft and slow. He curled into himself on the side of the road and waited to decay.

**RUBY HILTON** is a student and aspiring author. Her secondary schooling career was filled with building her fiction-writing skills and working towards publication. When not working on her first novel, she is reading Andrea Dworkin or watching her AFL team play: practising for her dream job in sports media.

# Love and Death and Treasures

S.G. McMahon

James woke up to a text message from his mother.

Call me when you're free

It was what she'd said when his boyhood dog had died. She'd sent the text only after the golden retriever had been cremated and was trapped inside a tiny wooden box.

He called his mother.

'Morning James. Your father didn't want to make a fuss, but he has cancer,' his mother said matter-of-factly. She didn't wait for him to respond. 'It's stage four prostate cancer. Stage four means it's in his bones. He started radiotherapy last week.'

'Oh.'

'Most of the doctors won't tell us how much longer he has left so that we can get a second opinion, but one doctor said it'll be about ten years if the radiotherapy works. Apparently prostate cancer is quite slow.'

'Is he going to retire?' James asked. His mother had become a messenger between them as of late. A habit that not even a cancer diagnosis could break.

'Yes, he thinks so.'

'Does he feel okay?'

'Yes, he feels fine. A bit zapped from the radiotherapy.'

'Should I come home?'

'No, don't bother, I know work is busy.'

'Okay, let me know if I need to come back and help with anything.'

'Will do. I love you, bye.'

'I love you too, Mum.'

James felt numb. Had his father ever told him 'I love you'? He searched for a memory – anything. His father had often told James that he was bright and kind and precocious, but never 'I love you'.

Then he made a coffee and went to work.

△ △ △

Time passed faster than it had any right to. Ten years became Eight. James didn't have enough leave accrued to go home and see his parents. It wasn't like when he was in university and could go home for the holidays.

Eight years became Five without James really noticing. His apartment was what he thought of as home now. His childhood home was his parents' house. And if he took vacation time to go there, it wouldn't be relaxing. James was pudgier around the middle now and saw his father when he looked in the mirror.

James's father died with Two years left to live.

He went home to help with the funeral and found that his mother had become an 'old person'. Frail. Her hair was whiter than he remembered and her walk slower.

When he looked into the coffin and saw his father, he found that his father had become an 'old person', too.

'Still got a full head of hair,' he congratulated the corpse.

△ △ △

His mother had a hobble. She said the stairs of their home were hard on her hip, so he helped sell the house and the ten acres attached. The new owners knocked the house down while his mother travelled interstate to move in with him.

'What's this?' he asked his mother. She supervised as he moved her things into his spare room. He held an old iron safe; it was ridiculously heavy.

'I don't know. Your father called them his treasures.'

He sat it down on the floor and twisted the dial. 2-6-0-3, the date of his parents' anniversary. His PIN for everything so he wouldn't forget. His mother peered over his shoulder as he sorted through the contents.

The safe contained old jewellery in a plastic bag designed to hold coins – probably his paternal grandmother's. She had always been horrible to her son. Why had he kept his mother's jewellery instead of selling it?

His father's birth certificate, dated 9 February 1951. He wouldn't have much use for that anymore.

There was a fat disk drive. The sort that probably would've cost hundreds of dollars in the early 2000s, but now looked like a brushed-metal brick. His mother seemed to recognise it.

The last item was a yellow piece of paper folded in half inside a plastic sleeve. James carefully extracted it. It was a report card from 1 November 1961. It said that Steven was 'a very bright young boy'. That he was 'kind and precocious' and was 'learning quickly'. The paper was frayed and rounded at the edges, like it had been read over and over.

△ △ △

The year went by and his mother insisted they put up a Christmas tree. She was a pain, but he remembered to be grateful she was there. He bought a Christmas tree and went to the Reject Shop for decorations. The ones from his childhood home had not survived the move.

He walked past the aisle of ornaments and over to the tinsel and felt deeply bad on the inside. Like something had curdled in his stomach, and hot and tight in the back of his throat. Like there was something sour in the middle of his brain.

He shoved some decorations into his basket. The tinsel stuck to his fingers. He shook it off, the scent of dust and synthetic foil hitting him like a punch to the gut. Inexplicably, he felt the urge to scream and wail like a child. Tears welled up in his eyes. He wanted to go back home, but home didn't exist anymore.

He rushed back to his apartment as quickly as possible and hugged his mum.

'Are you okay, love?' she asked.

'I don't know.' He ugly-cried, his face contorting without his consent.

'Sorry, I shouldn't have sent you out for the decorations.'

'What, why?'

'Have you looked at what was in the hard drive yet?'

'No?'

'I'll make you a cup of tea. Plug it into the telly.'

He did as he was told. 2-6-0-3, hard drive, TV. There were twenty-two video files, each carefully named and dated. One for every year.

1 December 1990. James was a baby in a cot that had been dragged out to the living room as his mother decorated the Christmas tree, his father giving directions from behind the camera.

1 December 1995. James was five and throwing tinsel up into the air, hoping it landed on the tree. His mother sat on the couch with a cup of tea and his father remained behind the camera, audio cutting out as his father laughed close to the microphone.

1 December 2005. He was fifteen and pretending to look like he was too cool to decorate the tree in front of his first girlfriend. His father had woken him up early on Christmas morning later that year, excited to see him unwrap his gifts.

25 December 2011. This was the last time James had bothered to come home for Christmas. A phone call, he'd thought after that, would do.

'Oh,' said James. Still, he wept. His father had said 'I love you'. Just in his own way.

**S.G. MCMAHON** is a Melbourne-based writer. They respectfully acknowledge the Wurundjeri People of the Kulin Nation, who are the Traditional Owners of the land on which they write, and pay their respect to their Elders past, present and emerging. S.G. McMahon is contactable at s.g.mcmahon1@gmail.com.

# From End to Beginning

Kayla Sinclair

*Content warning: this piece contains depictions of self-harm and disordered eating. Please read with care.*

It's November. You've been sixteen for six months. You're single for the first time in years, and while it was fun at first, now you just miss him. You still talk all the time, about everything, but mostly about sex. At the time of your break-up, you hadn't gone far, third base at most. But now you want more. You want to feel something, and you think maybe by doing this he might just fall in love with you again. But you're wrong – he's never really loved anyone.

It takes three weeks of constant pestering before you finally give in to him, and he tells you to come over. When you get there, you sneak around the side of the house and climb through his bedroom window because his parents have a security camera and he's grounded. There's no hello; he immediately gets to it. The first thing he does, after getting you to sit on the bed, is put on some music. It's the first song he ever showed you and it's one of your favourite bands. You think this means he must remember; maybe there's still a chance. But it's been ten months and there's no chance.

He won't kiss you, not properly. He doesn't want to show that sort of emotion, doesn't want you to think it's serious. He refuses to use protection, says it's too uncomfortable and it doesn't feel good and – seeing as it's your first time and you're too frightened of rejection to argue – you let it happen. Afterwards, you can't help but cry. You thought it would be different, you thought it might be romantic. You thought that maybe, just maybe, he'd want to get back together. But it wasn't, and he didn't.

He leaves the room for a moment, and while he washes up, you make yourself bleed. When he returns, you cover the cuts and he doesn't notice. He just tells you to go back out the same way you came in. Won't even kiss you goodbye. You walk to the bus stop crying and text your friend, knowing he'll be able to help. He's always been there when you've felt like doing something dumb, and you're still here now because of him, because of his kind words and his ability to convince you that stepping onto the road wasn't the way to go.

It's April. It's your sweet sixteenth and you're celebrating by having your friends over for a movie-themed party. You've invited your ex and found the sexiest costume you possibly could. You don't eat for three days so that you can look good in it, but you don't tell anyone. They just think you're wobbly because you're tired. He's promised to bring UDLs as a birthday gift, but drinks all six of them on his way from the station to your house.

He's brought a mutual friend for company, and they've walked 3 km in the rain to be here. You're happy to see him, and you think it means something that he got drunk and walked through the rain to see you.

At first, you're having fun. The boys are sitting on the couch. You're off dancing with your girlfriends. You look over and see him watching you, and, feeling brave, you decide to excuse yourself to sit between them. You put your hand on his thigh as he leans in and says you're looking good. Hearing him say that makes the pain worth it.

The night wears on and you start to feel the sadness creeping in. You distract yourself by sitting with him and resting your head on his shoulder. He puts an arm around your waist and tells you *whatever it is, you're strong enough to get through it*. You ask him how he could possibly know that, and he responds by saying *I know you*. He's right of course, and by the end of the night, you're back to normal, albeit slightly disappointed by the lack of alcohol in your system.

Seeing as he and his friend are the last people at the party, your father offers to drive them home, and you tag along. He's being dropped off last, so you sit in between them. He takes your hand and guides it over to his lap. From experience, you know what he's looking for and you oblige. Somewhere along the way, he leans into you and whispers that he feels bad his friend is missing out. He tells you to kiss him, and even though you're uncomfortable about the idea of kissing another guy; you're in love and will do anything he says. So, you do it.

After that night, he starts talking to you more often, and the conversations slowly transition from flirting to him asking when he can see you again. You're still in love and watch too many romantic comedies, so you think it's sweet that he wants to catch up, and you have it in your head that maybe 'catch up' is code for 'getting back together'.

It's January. You're fourteen and at a summer camp. You spend your days surrounded by the sounds of nature and the smell of eucalyptus. You play games and make t-shirts and have water balloon fights. At night, the leaders sing songs and you watch movies. When you're back in bed, you play silly games of truth or dare with your cabin buddies.

You meet a guy on the camp. He's sweet, shy and has an adorable accent. He knows you have issues from the first time you talk and he's okay with it. He asks if you're okay, and when you lie and say you're fine, he tells you he knows you're not, and then he holds your hand, turns it over and kisses your wrist. He's seen the scars hidden under your bracelets. It's a simple gesture, but to you it means the world.

You kiss him for the first time at the movie night and go with him to the camp gala, where he watches you all night to make sure you eat, since you haven't all week.

When camp's over, you continue to see each other. He meets your parents and you meet his. He tells you about his childhood, and shares secrets he's never told anyone else. You do the same, even though he technically already knows most of your secrets. He makes you happy, and he makes you even happier when, one day, he tells you he loves you, and he makes you a promise that he'll always be there, and he'll always care.

---

**KAYLA SINCLAIR** is an aspiring author who loves poetry and creative non-fiction. She is currently working on her first poetry collection and hopes to be published by the time she's thirty. She loves to read, and often enjoys perusing romance and young adult fantasy novels in her spare time.

# Martin and His Mother

Nik Anastassiades

Martin's mother was doing the dishes when he decided to drop the bomb. He'd dropped it a few times before. It always ended in the same fight. She stopped, looked at him and spoke sternly, 'Why do you need to know?'

'I just feel like I should have some sort of explanation,' he said.

'Your father left. There you go. Not much more to it. You know, it's pretty bloody offensive that you keep asking about this …' She shook her head and went back to her washing.

Martin pressed, 'I think it's pretty reasonable.'

'For fuck's sake, Martin! Who cares where he is?' She didn't make eye contact. Martin knew he'd have to tread lightly. His mother was known to throw a plate if provoked. Especially when doing the dishes.

'He left when you were born. I chucked him out,' she said.

'Yeah, you've said that, but why didn't you ever talk about it? Why's Dad a fuckin' enigma?'

'Because he's a dickhead,' she said, leaving the room and throwing a tea towel on the kitchen bench, the dishes still dirty. Martin followed her out of the kitchen. He was getting an answer, and he was getting it now. The subject of his father had been an elusive one his entire life.

'Martin, can you fuck off? I'm sick of being interrogated by my son.'

'Come off it, just tell me. Is he gay? Is he dead? Did he fuck someone younger? Did he cut his dick off in a trampolining accident? What happened?'

'He left, okay! Your dad wasn't ... well. He had issues. I told him to leave until he sorted them out ...' She stopped and planted herself on the couch in their lounge room. 'I always thought he'd come back after he did it. He never did. Never heard a word from him since.'

'Come back?' Martin asked.

'Yeah. Like ... like that Paul Kelly song.' She paused and sighed.

'Which Paul Kelly song?' he asked.

'Y'know, the one where the bloke's a drunk, and she pisses off to wherever, and then he sorts himself out.' She shook her head, 'Well it obviously *sounds* stupid, doesn't it?'

'Just a bit fuckin' stupid, yeah. But I guess ...'

'I wouldn't expect a child would understand it. You think you're grown up ... you're not.'

Martin had lots of things he wanted to say. *Where is he? Have you kept in touch? Can I meet him? Would he like to meet me?* But he didn't ask any of them. He looked at his mother. She looked like she might cry. Martin could tell it was hard for her to say what she said; she had never been this vulnerable in front of him before. He was beginning to understand why she'd never told him. He'd known his mother to be stern and confident – he didn't even *know* she was into Paul Kelly. It was definitely hard for her, even if he thought it *was* pretty fuckin' stupid that she thought her life would play out like that one, very specific, Paul Kelly song.

He sat by his mother on the couch, and he held her. Things change; people change.

She smiled at their embrace. He could see she was happy that her son would try to understand, even if his understanding was limited. She got up to finish the dishes.

'Where are you going? To the door?' He smiled.

'Fuck off, Martin.'

'Get it, because the song's called "To her door".' He sniggered.

'Yes, I got it.' She left the room.

**NIK ANASTASSIADES** is an emerging writer from Melbourne. Nik has produced a screenplay for a childrens TV series, *Jar dwellers SOS*. He is currently working on a young adult novel, 'Kinda Like an Albatross'. In his spare time, Nik writes, directs and edits short films and sketch comedy. You can find him on Instagram @nik.pix.

# The Doctor

## Nompumelelo Mpehle

It is midmorning by the time Dr Dea Throe returns from work. Entering her house from the garage, she finds her retired mother in the living room snoring on the couch with the TV on. Her daughter sits on the staircase to her right with a toy doctor's kit at her side, pretending to listen to the make-believe organs in a shaggy brown teddy bear's belly with a plastic stethoscope. She removes the earpieces and puts a hand to her chin thoughtfully.

Dea closes her eyes and cycles through her memories of the past twenty-four hours, where she used the professional versions of the tools in that kit to slice open, pull out and stitch in, until her hands were soaked in blood that peeled off easily when the latex gloves were removed. She submerges herself into the memories for a bit, then lets them drain away.

Her daughter notices her as she approaches the stairs but doesn't move. She's taking up the whole thoroughfare, and Dea is so tired from her obscenely long hours – if only her daughter could scoot aside and let her past instead of just staring at her.

'Sea, sweetie —' is all Dea gets out before Sea asks:

'Can we play now? You promised that we'd play once you got back.'

There is nothing Dea wants to do less, but she remembers that promise. Or was it the promise before? Or the one before that? How many times has she made that promise? So instead, she smiles and sits down on the step beside her daughter. 'Sure. What's wrong with Mr Teddy, Dr Sea?'

Sea clucks her tongue. 'My patient's name is Mr Beartolomeo Ursarus. He's sick. Clearly.'

Dea sighs through her nose and tries to keep a straight face. 'Do you know what's wrong with him yet?'

Sea shakes her head.

'That bad, huh?'

Sea nods.

'Don't worry, I'm sure we can fix him up. Let's go to the bathroom and see if we have any medicine that might help.'

'Oh no, it's already gone far beyond that,' Sea says grimly. 'Mr Ursarus is going to need surgery. My only concern is that I don't have a nurse to give the patient the quality care he needs.'

'I just got off my shift – I don't have much time to play,' Dea explains.

'Medical care is not a game. I app-ree-shi-pate your help until I find a proper nurse, but I need you to de-mon-ster-ate that you're going to be serious.' Sea picks up her teddy bear and passes it to Dea. 'To assess your trust-iness, you shall carry the patient to his bed. I'll show you to his room.'

Sea puts her stethoscope away and carries her doctor's kit up the stairs. Dea fights the pressure of exhaustion in her eyelids as she cradles the teddy in one arm and grabs her briefcase with the other, bringing it with her as Sea takes them to her bedroom. It's tidy and blue, themed around seashells and mermaids. Sea takes them to the end of her bed where a makeshift clinic has been set up, consisting of a child-sized table with a white cloth thrown over the top.

'Please lay the patient down carefully,' Sea instructs, pointing at the table. 'We're now going to operate.' She puts her doctor's kit down beside the table. Dea kneels beside the table and does as she's told, while Sea reaches beneath the cloth to take out an unlabelled aerosol can. Dea frowns.

'Sea, what's that?'

'Teddy bear gas,' Sea answers nonchalantly and sprays liberally into the teddy's face. 'Count backwards from ten, Mr Ursarus.'

The spray smells slightly of peonies, but nothing instantly concerning to Dea, so she allows Sea to continue until she deems the teddy sufficiently passed out and puts the can down. The next thing she does is reach into her doctor's kit and pull out a large sharp pair of metal scissors. Dea's eyes widen.

'Where did you get those?' she barks.

'I'm a doctor and I got this from a le-git-im-bate medical company,' Sea answers. Dea is too tired to comprehend that nonsense before Sea has begun to cut her teddy bear open, straight up the middle. Instead of fluff, however, the inside of this bear looks distinctly slimy and pink. 'We'll need to take a good look inside.'

To Dea's horror, she produces a scalpel from her doctor's kit. A *real* scalpel. A real, professional scalpel that was definitely not in there when Dea bought the kit at Toyworld.

'No, no, absolutely not!' She reaches for the tool but Sea brandishes the impeccably sharp end a bit too recklessly. Where could she have possibly gotten it?

'I'm going to open up the heart,' Sea declares. She reaches into the mess of squishy stuff and pulls out a heart. An actual heart. It's far too big for the teddy bear, even if it had been alive. It slices open like fresh flesh and strange black things are poking out of the vents – spiders. Little black plastic spiders. 'Uh oh! The heart got filled with spiders. No wonder Mr Ursarus is so afraid all the time.'

Dea looks at her daughter. Really looks at her. 'Afraid? What are you afraid of?'

'I'm not afraid,' Sea replies a little too emphatically. 'This is Mr Ursarus's operation. He's afraid. I think someone he loved left and didn't come back. So, now he's going to be alone forever.'

Dea's heart feels achy and hollow. Sea has always been sensitive, but to imagine a surgical removal of loneliness? Who else could have caused such grief but the parent who didn't come home enough? 'I see. Well, let's take away the fear he has right now.' Just to keep playing along, she adds, 'And afterwards, we'll give him some courage pills to manage his fear. His loved one wants to come back, but she's so busy. She's helping other people the same way you're helping him. But in case something goes really wrong, let's give him a treatment plan to help him find some friends who can love him just as much.'

Dea tries looking at the teddy again, but her exhausted eyes don't catch the details of Mr Ursarus's spider-infested heart, making her wonder if the grizzly sight is real. Sea holds the heart, sliced open and pulled out. But between them there are no ideas on how to stitch the love back in. Dea's best offer is to say, 'I'm sure he'll be okay. After all, he's got a great doctor.'

---

As a poet, **NOMPUMELELO MPEHLE** explores down-to-earth topics like politics, culture and nature. As a prose writer, she spins wild tales of fantasy and science fiction. Nompumelelo will write just about anything. She's been an MC, a college magazine editor, a performance poet and a legal document editor.

# Pill

### Madeline Crehan

*I think it will be good for us—*

*us,*
he'd said
but libido slowed, mood plateaued
until it was just me and her:
the body.

The change slow at first,
her pain began to ease,
manufactured clockwork
      reliability.

Ovaries' wrath subdued
      for now
out of bed when I bled,
discomfiting comfort.

She curved and swelled
hips widened, ready for
impossible child,
tricked by her creator.

Tinier than tic tacs
convenient,
peace of mind—
mind at war.

Sexless weeks turn sexless months,
lack of pain eclipsed by
lack of pleasure;
she's allowed both or neither.

⚠ ⚠ ⚠

Turning away from her
        I dive into myself
                drowning
                        too deep for the moon to
                                find me.

⚠ ⚠ ⚠

Pill-free I'm coming up
for air above the swell,
finding my feet on land again,
tide returning to its steady rhythm.

I feel her pain
waves        blood        body
feel her pleasure too
soft        warm        heavy.

Her stretch marks map
the path her hair follows,
reaching for the earth,
roots entwined with body.

△ △ △

Grounded
                I bloom
                        as
                                the new moon
                                        welcomes Spring.

---

**MADELINE CREHAN** is a writer, reader and feminist based in
Naarm/Melbourne. Her writing explores gender, grief and mental
health and has been published with *ABC News*, rosie.org.au and
whynot.org.au. Madeline is the Marketing and Programming
Manager at *Kill Your Darlings*. Find her work at madelinecrehan.com
and @madelinecrehan on Instagram.

# The Poisoning of the Babe

TC Nagy-Felsobuki

This excerpt is the inciting incident from
a long-form novel, 'The Lantern Lighters'.

Lux the Saviour Child sleeps serenely in a cot hanging on carefully corded ropes. Sweet honeyed breezes rock her gently to and fro, and from the windowsill a nightingale trills lullaby, as soothing as the tones of a lightly strummed harp. Even in slumber, Lux's expression holds her blessing smile.

But dark denials are a-scuttle. The nightingale's song abruptly ceases and the air holds its perfumed breath. Up and over the windowsill – delineating the outside world and the room where the babe sleeps – scuttles an onyx-shaded, nine-eyed, mense spider, silent as graven. It is an affront, in its blackness, against the pristine white-paint framing of the window, the room and the sleeping child within.

The spider climbs the wall with ease, till hemmed by join of wall and ceiling, which it traverses. It makes its way upside-down along the sturdy truss beam from which swings Lux's cot. When the spider is directly above the babe, it ignores the cradling ropes and lets itself rapidly down on a thread of its own spinning.

⟁ ⟁ ⟁

At this same instant, a new actor enters the scene. 'Huzzah!' It is ik – Wynkyn de Sward. 'Stande ho fowrl bane!'[1] cry ik, darting through the open window, my sword drawn from the sheath and upraised in hand.

The babe awakens, smiles, and stretches her innocent fingers towards the black mass dangling over her.

'Nix, lyte maid-child,' cry ik. 'Nix!'[2]

But it is too late. The babe giggles and my wicked foe, that ghastly creature, hovers above her palm and grips her tiny thumb. Dart ik and thrust my sword into the middlemost of his nine hideous orbs, which blazes red, but halts him not. He rears those spindle-elbow legs and spits. Though dodge and weave ik, a venomous droplet flicks my hind-wing and burns a hole right through, rapid as acid.

Drastically un-aerodynamicked – plunge ik out of the very firmament that upholds moi no longer – within sight of the malevolent beast sinking its sharp fangs into the babe's soft thumb flesh and injecting his coma-inducing poison. The surprised babe yowls like the banshee as the poison races straight to her heart. The quoll rushes in, the spider retracts its web-thread, and fall ik to the ground, knocking unconscious myself.

In my temporary absence from the daily affairs of this Byhelios world, dream ik of LaFée, my soul's utmost love and precious treasure. In my dream, we are together again in Limerance, in the garden of The Temple of Our Hearts. My joy is great: thus, greatly chagrins me her gentle admonishment.

'Was not ever impetuositee the challenge of the warrior

Beterfflye striving for the Light, Wynkyn de Sward?'[3] she reminds me, as we flute the air, wingtip-to-wingtip.

△ △ △

The advent of Petrus the quoll saves Wynkyn de Sward's life in this moment. The babe's startled cry summons the Lightheart family's pet just as the dread spider is about to spring from thread to puncture and poison, with festered fangs, the unconscious Beterfflye, Wynkyn.

On instinct the quoll stands shield over the fallen Beterfflye, snarling and snapping, questing with eyes, ears and sensitive nose to detect the reason for disturbance.

Malintento, dangerously aware of the omnivorous nature of quolls – as ready to crunch up an enormous spider as a diet of berries and leaves – releases Lux's tiny throbbing thumb and retracts hastily.

The quoll rushes him, but the spider retreats higher still, scurrying nimbly back up its rope of coarse-spun thread. Petrus leaps high, teeth champing, but Malintento reaches safer haven in the rafters and crouches there, nursing his bloody eye: waiting.

△ △ △

Lux's yowl, sharp and vivid against the tranquil atmosphere of the day, has scythed Lunella's concentration. Never before has so anguished a wail been uttered by her sunshine-natured baby sister. Dropping both chunk of wood and tool from hand, Lunella races out of Luceat's workshop where, when she should have been minding the babe, she has been immersed instead, practising turning sabots. She gains the house, wrenches open the door and skeeters inside.

Petrus, bristles on end, stands over something lying on the floor. Lunella leaps beyond the quoll to reach her sister and leans over the stilled cot. Any heart must be wrenched at the sight of sweet Lux's tear-streaked face, and the little one reaches her arms out, seeking comfort and reassurance. Lunella gently lifts her up and holds her close, petting and soothing the babe, even while she scans the room, trying to make sense of the seen and the unseen. If only quolls could talk.

Lux hiccups a sob. Then another. Lunella pats her back and jiggles her very gently; anything to distract the child from her distress. Lux rests her tiny cheek against Lunella's shoulder and the older sister croons a sea-shanty. Centuries-old, still sung by the women of Anchor-by-Sea to enchant their fishermen husbands, sons and sweethearts home from the oceans – hearty, hale and safe.

Presently the babe soothes and grows drowsy. Determined to keep her close now, Lunella wraps her in a swaddle, then twines the material around her own torso. Lux is cocooned in the soft fabric sling across her sister's back, where, heartbeat-to-heartbeat, Lunella will protect Lux from further terror. But the question of what caused the babe to cry so sharply hangs in the air as if spoken aloud.

Lunella runs seeking hands over the framing of the cot and under the quilt and the bedding. Petrus snouts insistently towards the ceiling but when Lunella leans back to look up she cannot spy anything there amiss. For the spider, retreated to the loft space high overhead, is simply a black mass indistinguishable from the overall lofty gloom.

Lunella bends to peer underneath Lux's cot and Petrus steps aside, revealing some misshapen creature, the specie of which is unrecognisable at first quick scan. What is obvious though is a sword, drawn free of scabbard, with fiercely-honed blade and bloodied point still gripped mortis-tightly in the creature's hand.

By the full force of the Divine Mysterium, under witness of the refraction of the twin Byhelian suns – if this creature has harmed her sister – Lunella will rip off its armour, tear its six limbs from its body, and smite head from neck with its own sword.

---

[1] 'Huzzah!' It is I. 'Stand ho foul demon!' I yell.
[2] 'No, little babe,' I yell. 'No!'
[3] 'Is not impetuosity the challenge of the warrior Beterfflye striving for the Light, Wynkyn de Sward?'

---

**TC NAGY-FELSOBUKI** is an emerging writer of marvellous and spiritual realism. Trace is an enthusiastic weaver of fascinating words. She is immersed in the invention of Butterflorian, a novel language for her work 'The Lantern Lighters', and has three articles published by invitation on PWE's *Cardigan Street*.

# Generation Pessimism

## Caitlin Goh

This is an excerpt from a larger work.

I lay on the hard wooden floor. As I felt my body fighting to stay alive, I wondered how I could have unleashed this on myself. You spend all this time thinking no-one will fight to save you, and in your most desperate moments you find you fighting for yourself. My heart beat faster by the second and I gasped for air. This was the end. My body was shutting down bit by bit and I would finally be free. Wasn't that what I wanted?

I wanted to run from the abandoned house to find help. To scream for someone. To undo what I had done. I rolled onto my stomach. I remembered the story of a forgotten Hollywood starlet, Carole Landis, who killed herself. She was found facedown on the kitchen floor with her arms bent under her as if she had tried to lift herself one final time but couldn't. That was the fate that would befall me. I tried to lift myself off the floor. I collapsed and let out a desperate sob.

Eventually, my heart slowed. Eternity no longer felt painful.

Familiar scenes and faces began to flicker before me.

Mum. Dad. Ava. Daniel. Hassan.

Birthdays. Graduations. Holidays. First love. The smaller memories in life that get ignored. Family movie nights. Childhood playtime.

When I first found this hut.

I ran. From Singapore to Australia to Turkey. To all over Europe at one point. I ran physically. I ran emotionally. I ran from a problem that was inside me all along. It was a parasite I couldn't kill. But it was fun running from it.

Memories flashed faster and faster. Light slowly absorbed all the images of the past until there was nothing but light left. The light morphed into a tunnel and I sped through it.

I made my way to a forest. There were no paths. No sign of human intervention in the forest. The ground was a soft mix of dirt and rotting bark and leaves. Beams of sunlight shone down through the tops of the ancient trees, their trunks a patchwork of moss and bark. At the base of the trees there were fern bushes. Wildflowers spotted the forest floor, offering pops of vivid pink, yellow, blue, purple, orange and red, cutting through the shades of green and brown. Their sweet floral scents mixed perfectly with the woodsy aroma.

I began to walk and the light mist that hung in the air dampened my skin. It was fresh, like dawn.

I stepped into a field of wheat baked in golden sunlight. The mist disappeared and the sunlight warmed my skin. A gentle breeze swayed the wheat stalks and rustled the leaves of the trees at the edge of the forest behind me. I held out my hands, palms and fingers extended, and let the wheat tickle my fingertips as

I walked. The dirt was soft, devoid of any of the dangers that you get warned about in life like sharp objects or deadly bugs. It powdered my feet and I slowly spun around as I drifted through the field.

This was it. The end.

**CAITLIN GOH** is a freelance writer and editor. She has placed in several international screenplay competitions, including winning the Silver Award at the Independent Shorts Awards in Los Angeles, May 2022. She is interested in writing fiction of all genres. Caitlin can be found at caitlingoh.com.au.

# Life, Death and the Bush

### Lindy Ralph

'I hope Bubba's not dead,' I joke to Elvis as we speed down our dusty driveway, praying we make it to the school bus on time. 'Rocky was barking early this morning and Bubba didn't calm him down. I'll check on him when I get back.' Elvis, Dad and I are a close trio; underneath the joking is arcane fear.

△ △ △

Dad declared himself 'Bush Baptist'. The bush was his church, he said. Every single day he went for a walk with our little red dog, Rocky. If I was home when he got back, he'd tell me which hill or gully he'd traversed. Sometimes he showed me something he'd found, like a speck of gold from the road or a striking leaf.

He'd formed a group called Friends of the Box Ironbark. The scrubby new-growth trees grew all over our property out of the desolate land left by the gold rush. He fought to save the giant box ironbark that had survived. Ancient sentries of the Dja Dja Wurrung land, whispering their secrets as he lay between their mighty roots. Just 'thinking'.

⟁ ⟁ ⟁

This isn't the first time I've done a proof-of-life check on Dad; it's kind of a family joke. When Dad was twelve, his father dropped dead from a heart attack as he was opening a gate. Just like that. Gone in an instant. When he was fourteen, his mum died from a stroke. When he was seventeen, his brother died in a car accident.

If I hadn't seen him for a few days, I'd wander over to his house next door, only to find him sitting in his leather recliner, reading a book or listening to Radio National. 'Oh, you're alive,' I'd say. 'Yep,' he'd chuckle.

⟁ ⟁ ⟁

As I walk the path between my place and his, the cicadas remind me how hot it's going to be. Dad's mudbrick cottage – a former potting shed – is on the top left-hand corner of a quarter-acre plot of garden. It's fenced off from the rest of the property to keep the foxes and rabbits out. On the other side, slightly uphill, is the old chook shed where Rocky's locked up.

As I round the corner of his cottage, like I have thousands of times, it feels different. An unsettling stillness.

I creep onto the small wooden deck; the flywire door is open. I lean forward and see Dad lying on his side on the red-brick floor. He has his back to me, curled around the armchair in the corner. His head is behind the door. His desk chair has fallen on the floor. Instinctively I know not to look closer. He's fully clothed, wearing bottle-green trackpants and a long-sleeved shirt. He's wearing hiking boots. He always spends money on good boots.

I'm sucked into an alternate universe. He's dead. But is he? I lean in. His body is puffy, an overstuffed scarecrow fallen from its post. How long has he been here? When did I last see him? Was it four days ago? Five?

Suddenly I feel a force rise from the earth. Ancient, animalistic. It enters my body and pushes me back, stealing my breath. It's dark and roiling and powerful. It throws my head back. Black and grey and brown mist spews out as I scream.

I see the agony from outside my body. I'm hovering above and to the left. My neck arches back, exposing my throat, pure base pain pouring out into the bush.

The cicadas are silent. The dog has stopped barking. Birds and snakes and rabbits and possums freeze.

Thank fuck Elvis is at school. The sound I make is terrifying.

He's dead. I saw him, and I can smell it. The pungent, earthy smell that seeps into the car from the side of the highway in summer.

He's not in his body, but I feel him lingering in the trees. His essence.

I'm stumbling around the corner, near the geranium plants, hyperventilating. I need oxygen. I can't think.

The pain is trying to pull me down, forcing me to fold over like a fetus.

I'm staring at my phone. I can't remember how to use it. It's a nightmare. Something snaps and I call Triple Zero. There are too many options: police, ambulance, fire. I don't know. Police? Ambulance? I can't speak. My body is contorting; my breath is gone. They're sending police.

Fuck. Fuck. Fuck. FUCK.

I need someone. I call our friend Sandy; he lives on the other side of the hill.

Minutes later, Sandy is making tea because that's what you do. I'm not a tea drinker, but I take it.

Mum's on her way with Elvis and my younger brother. Someone calls my older brother in the city, and he's on his way too.

Finally, the police arrive.

'When was the last time you saw him?'

I don't know. When was it? What have I been doing? Today is Tuesday. On Friday, Elvis was diagnosed with Crohn's disease. Why didn't I go over and tell Dad?

Fuck.

Could it have been four days? Why didn't I go and see him? How long has he been dead?

FUCK.

Dad's GP turns up with a student doctor; they're here to pronounce him dead. When they come back, the doctor is tearing up. He says that he believes Dad had a massive heart attack and died instantly.

Just fell off his chair.

I imagine what they must have seen. Ants. Flies.

Next, the undertakers arrive. I don't want anything to do with it. Someone else meets them outside. When they're finished, they knock on the door.

'I'm really sorry, but you won't be able to have a viewing.'

I know it's because of what they saw behind the door.

It's seven years later, and I still don't know how long he lay dead while we were living our lives next door. The doctor told me I couldn't have saved him. I don't know. But there are two things I do know:

I'm glad I didn't look behind the door.

I will always feel him suspended in the wind as it whispers through the trees.

**LINDY RALPH** is a freelance writer and editor. She writes revealing non-fiction and has had work published on *ABC Everyday*, *Gippslandia* and *Mamamia*. Lindy loves scouring Melbourne's back streets to find high-quality cheap eats to share on her Instagram, @melbfoodexplorer. She can be found at lindyralph.com.au.

# The Landlord Special

## Maddox Gifford

The flat is largely unremarkable.

Popcorn ceiling. Grainy grey carpeting. Off-white walls with a wetness about them, the textured thickness of countless slapdash coats of paint: the landlord special.

The only saving grace is the window. Wide-stretched across the longest wall, waist-height wooden sill powdered with flaking white paint and deep enough to prop a hip against, or hop atop to perch precariously on. Seems a good spot for looking up at the stars. Or, during the day, down to the road below. The steady stream of cars, doppler-ripples humming as they pass.

You've paid more for worse; you've been rejected for better.

You sigh, and ask how to apply.

Your final arrival is a halting stagger under the heft of a damp-edged cardboard box. The brittle strip of masking tape says *bits n bobs*; upon opening it, you unearth a treasure-trove of lone socks and long-lost kitchenware.

Most of the boxes are already half-arsedly unpacked, the remainder pushed into corners; the room feels discomfitingly bare. Negative space beneath your feet. Ridged depressions from absent furniture, carpet compressed no longer.

After spending the afternoon hours absently rubbing your thumb along those lingering lines in coarse carpet, you venture onto the streets. There's always something to find outside, at least.

The very first corner you round reveals an alcove, concrete-shielded against the elements, that yields a haphazard scattering of furniture. A set of drawers only slightly too small to fit all your clothes; a sturdy couch, worse for wear but comfortable, functional; a banged-up table just shitty enough to avert obsessive stress over its future condition.

You drag and shuffle and hip-check each piece back to the flat, one by one. Somehow you are unsurprised to find them nestling neatly, easily, into the impressions left in the carpet. A perfect fit.

△ △ △

*The first night passes in a daze of dense peripherals, hazy outlines as yet unfamiliar. Tossing and turning scant centimetres above the floor, on the sunken mattress you'd been surprised to find propped up against the bathroom door ... There's something inside of it, you realise. Jumbled structures of some sort, almost recognisable, yet ultimately elusive. In the morning, you notice nothing amiss.*

△ △ △

Sun-shards splitting apart, distorting, distracting from the unshakably stale air. Less depressing with sunlight's illumination.

Precious little of that now, though. The cold comes on quick ... along with that familiar malignant creep of black mould, around the shower and in sinks, of which you are never fully rid.

You take to scrubbing every surface in reach, during each shower, never sure whether the light-headedness hitting halfway through is due to chemicals in cleaning solutions, or to having inhaled some of those deep-rooted mould spores that must have taken hold so long ago, never quite eradicated.

The pockmarked, filmy white walls become intolerable. You try putting up posters, and art prints, and picture frames: blu tack peels away in seconds, safe-stick hooks pop free instantly.

The more force you apply, the less likely these adhesives are to cooperate, so you soon stop trying.

You go out.

Not all nights, but most. There's always a special somewhere.

Cheaper, perhaps, to pre-drink at home. Only, you can't bear to just sit there, forcing yourself not to stare at those warped white walls.

So you head out when the sun sets. Stumble home as close to sunrise as seems feasible. Sleep away each subsequent day.

You aren't alone, some nights. A glint in the eye, a hand on the hip ... suddenly, you'll have company. A boy with wide gauges; a girl in winter-proof knee-high boots; a punk with well-frayed patches, peeling in places, strewn across a denim jacket that strains against taut shoulders.

You have them hold you, hold you down, hold you tight against the windowsill while you dig fingertips into the wall that borders the bathroom door, fists clenching, tensing, pretending paint isn't crumbling from corners beneath the pressure, only to spend those obligatory lazy mornings-after alone and intent on scraping every paint fragment from beneath your fingernails.

Whatever the reason, no lover ever lingers long.

Always your place. Theirs is always too far. Although you don't much like the area, you're becoming insular; this place finally feels safe, sometimes, and such familiarity trumps the truer freedom of open space.

*You can't really remember much, now: your old houses, your prior suburbs, your erstwhile lives ...*

Bugs. One: a lone, tiny thing. Then more, seemingly sudden swarms.

Roaches, possibly? Quite unlike any you've yet seen, in your years of renting.

You begin palm-sweeping your body and bedding at night, and each day upon waking.

The landlord calls.

Well, the agency does, actually (you've never even heard a landlord's voice) and proposes a longer-term lease.

You'll consider it, you say.

You won't; surely they know.

You hang up.

*You've been dreaming. Actual dreams again, your first in years ... First they take your flesh. The bugs come then. Skin from bone.*

*Stripped clean ... Extermination ... Not theirs. Fragile bones freed. Rattling within rotting walls. Slimy strokes coating ravaged skin ...*

△ △ △

A nap in a rare patch of sunlight. Floor-sprawled, hair carpet-tangled. You lie still there awhile.

You awaken to sensations of sinking, of struggling free ...

It takes some time, afterwards, to persuade yourself that it was only carpet in which you were ensnared, and only by your hair.

Bugs get into the food. Appetite annihilated, you hardly notice, floating on a safe hollow ache.

Have you been eating? It's irrelevant; they'll get it all eventually.

Freezing, fog-dense night.

You feel fingertips, trailing along your spine. You strip the mattress bare; nothing there.

Your back itches, shivers, twitches. Knife drawn, you tear into bloated bedding ... The *smell*. Trinkets tumble free, those precious little nothings that nobody would leave behind. Not willingly.

Then something clinks, falls from the slit. Vaguely cylindrical; smooth; eggshell-white.

Stronger than shell, though ... Or, well, so you'd thought; some of these are shattered. Intact pieces tumble out onto piled-up dust and crushed phalanges. You cringe at the reminder of how very breakable a body is.

Bit of a brittle building material, bone.

*They're inside the walls, you're sure of it. They'll come for you soon.*

Clawing; crumbling white walls; coming away with wet clumps. So close ... what awaits within?

*Sticky, acrid, sealing you in. Spoiled-milk-white. Glaring-fluorescent-white. Bone-white. Gone.*

Refracted light on barren white. A sparse apartment, with few redeeming features, but for the thrown-open window. A thin crowd, milling about, looking and touching but not listening ... not closely enough to hear, not nearly. A patched-up mattress propped against the dimpled wall. Deep furrows in dingy carpet each with its perfect match right round the corner.

Fingertips find a faint protrusion, tracing almost-familiar shapes in thick white paint.

---

**MADDOX GIFFORD** is a queer, neuroses-riddled writer and editor, and activist first and foremost, living (and sporadically thriving) in Naarm, by the beloved Merri Creek. Maddox's first year of life was spent on a rainforest reserve in NSW, and two subsequent decades predominantly on Worimi and Awabakal lands, a reluctant Novacastrian.

# Sasha

## Sarah Haines

This is an excerpt from a larger work, 'Sasha Raynes'.

It's the last Friday of the holidays and I'm panicking, rummaging through my wardrobe in search of an outfit for Year 11 on Monday. I need to look good now that I won't be forced to wear a school uniform. Clothes are strewn across the room, creating the illusion that I have lots of options but, really, I can't find a damn thing.

White t-shirt? Nah, it's going to be hot on Monday. I can't have visible sweat patches on my first day.

Black t-shirt? Nah, black will attract heat and make me sweat even more than normal.

Beige linen dress? Cute, but hell no. I'll have pit and back sweat marks.

I'd love to be one of those girls whose outfit choices weren't dictated by being a sweaty beast, but alas, I was born to perspire excessively.

My hand grazes the floral top I got at the Boxing Day sales. I've only worn it once: when Maddie and I went shopping in the city. It was hot that day but no sweat marks – done. I chuck my jeans on the floor – too hot for those. But a skirt could work. I trace my fingers down the folded edges of a wardrobe shelf, yank out a black skirt and try it on in front of the mirror.

Cute but not too cute. Legs out. Top nicely hugs my boobs. This is good. We like this. But what shoes? Sandals perhaps? I slide my feet into a pair on the floor nearby. Nah, too dressy. I'd rather be more casual than overdressed.

I retrieve my Converse sneakers from underneath my bed, chuck them on and go back to the mirror.

This is it. This is my first day of Year 11 outfit. Sasha Raynes: sweat free, carefree and comfortably shoed. This is how I'm going to be introduced to my peers. I take a mirror selfie before crashing onto my bed. Maybe I'll find *my* people in college. By my people, I mean people who love reading and writing and hate PE. Thank fuck we don't have to do PE anymore. My friends are great but for some strange reason they all love playing sport.

Lying on my belly, the pit of my stomach churns. What if I don't make any friends in college? I mean, heaps of people from high school are going to Canberra College, including Maddie, but what if I don't make any new friends and get left behind? I'm sure I'm worrying for no reason. Hopefully I'll make stacks of new friends including hot guys who think I'm hot too. Hopefully some of those hot guys fancy me and ask me out.

I can't believe I'm starting college without ever having a boyfriend. Mortifying. By sixteen, most people have had at least one serious relationship. Maddie has had several. Everyone else from our friend group has too. And lost their virginities. Me? None. Nil. Naught. Why have I never had a boyfriend? What the heck is wrong with me? Why have I only had three people ask me out in my life? In Year 5 it was Danny Milton, who still kissed his mum on the lips when she dropped him off for school. Year 8 it was Jacob Akers who was a total dero who stole stuff from school bags and picked fights with everyone. And last year it was Billy Chen who was actually pretty hot, but that died after our bowling date where we argued furiously about bumpers.

Sometimes I wonder if I've never had a boyfriend because I'm half Filipino. In Year 7, I had the hots for Mitchell Hack. We had drama together and one of his friends overhead Maddie and me talking about him and told Mitchell that I fancied him.

Shortly after, Mitchell called me into the hallway. 'I'm not into Asians,' he said, then ran back to his friend.

I was completely humiliated and heartbroken that he didn't like me because of my race. I went home and cried to Heather, but she wouldn't have it.

'Fuck that little racist shit, he's not worth your tears. You need to call him out on it because little racist shits turn into big racist shits and that's far worse.' She pepped me up with insults I could use and together we workshopped a comeback.

The next day in drama, I called Mitchell into the hallway. Reading from the notes I'd made on the palm of my hand, I began: 'I will not tolerate bigotry and prejudice from a little red nook like you.'

'What? Red nook? What's that?'

Nerves had caused my palms to sweat and smudge the writing. I squinted at my palm. 'Oh sorry. Neck. Little redneck like you,' I continued. 'Hack by name, hack by reputation. Bitch.' The addition of 'bitch' was entirely my own improv.

He scratched his head, 'Huh?'

'What you said yesterday was shitty. And racist.'

He turned red and laughed nervously. 'Sorry ... that you're pissed.' He ran back into the classroom before I could respond, and we never spoke again.

The Mitchell incident was a long time ago, but I still think about it every time I have a crush on someone.

Perhaps the reason I've never had a boyfriend is simpler than that – maybe I'm just ugly? I take another selfie and assess it. My hair is fantastic – shiny and long enough to cover my nips if I found myself in a situation where I didn't have access to a shirt. My skin is good, I rarely get pimples and it's a nice, tanned shade with freckles on top. I've got a good face too, awesome cheekbones. I'm a massive cutie. And I need to find someone who appreciates that. My phone buzzes.

**Maddie**
Hey bitch! Sleepover at mine tomorrow? Last one before we officially become college girls

**Me**
Sounds good!

I send Maddie the mirror selfie.

**Me**
First day of college outfit. Thoughts?

**Maddie**
😍🐥🔥
There's hope for you not dying a
virgin yet!

**Me**
🖕

---

**SARAH HAINES** is a writer working on her first manuscript.
By night, she writes fiction and has a penchant for writing humour.
By day, she writes non-fiction in her communications role at
Creative Victoria.

# Open Palm

Emma Hearnes

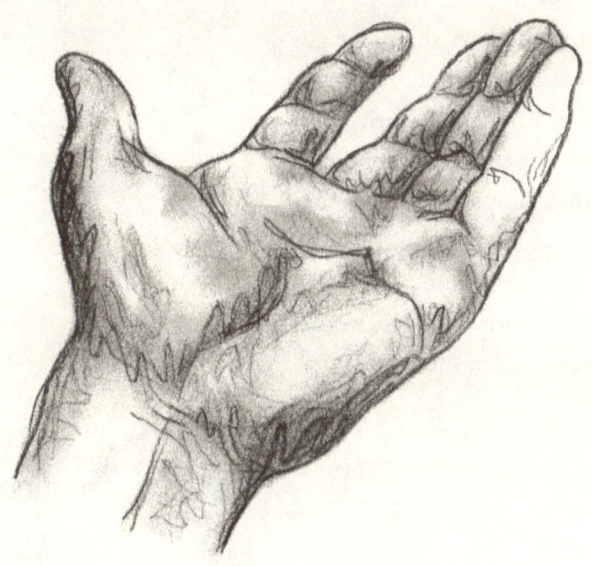

my mother is the open palm
she taught me that good girls
outstretch their fingers
offer up their heart line
anything you have should be given
hand it all out and take
whatever you get in return
carry their pain like a promise
hold their hurt with your breath
and if it all starts to spill
from that open palm
remember your shoulders were built
for the weight of the world

my mother is the open palm
she taught me how to whisper
closed fists into opening
undress hand-me-down hurt
she said we are all within reach
of being the people
we have washed our hands of
count your blessings on your fingers
hold your thanks with your breath
it is a privilege to show someone
the back of their own hand
to point them in the direction
of themselves

*Image by Emma Hearnes*

**EMMA HEARNES** called herself an artist until all her artworks became poems and she enrolled in PWE. Now she is an artist, a poet, a creative non-fiction writer and an editor – currently completing an editorial internship at *Gippslandia* magazine. For pen and paintbrush updates, follow her on Instagram @emmahearnes.

# Lone Tree

## P.K. Brookes

I started as a seed. Planted in a pot by sticky, sticky fingers. The pot was painted with red and yellow and green, all tiny dots, made in a fete stall. I watched the smile of the small human with coil-blonde curls and marshmallow cheeks as they buried me in dirt.

It was dark. So dark, for so long. I tunnelled through the darkness for weeks. Only the sounds of running feet on pavement and the stories of the Little One's adventures to guide me.

The outside world was bright and warm; a happy shiver ran down my spine when I finally emerged from the cocoon of soil. When I peeked over the edge of the pot, I saw Little One run under the legs of a taller human and run around the yard. I saw them shriek with joy when they noticed my small green sprout. Little One grinned, flashing their picket-fence teeth.

I grew taller. So did Little One. But the Big One stayed the same.

I grew more leaves. I became tall enough to see over the pot edge easily. When I could see a window above me, but not through it, I would wait for Little One to come outside. The sun was getting less warm and less bright, but Little One would warm me up with their praise.

'Look, it's bigger,' Little One would point and show Big One.

*So are you*, I would think. They smiled, revealing a gap in their fence. They sprinkled me with water. Splash, splash. And then Little One was whisked off into a big red car. Then I would wait. And wait some more. Watching the fuzzy bees collecting yellow fluff and leaving it across the other plants. The bees didn't come to me, I would just watch from afar. Then, with the rumble of the ground, I would know Little One was home.

They did this day after day. Little One would come home with a bag filled to the top with colourful paper and a sleepy face.

The world got colder, the sun got much less bright, and night would allow ice to form at my fingers. I saw Little One less and less; they spent less time outside with me. I stood there for days, waiting, only seeing glimpses of them as they dashed in and out of house and car.

Finally, the world grew warm and bright once more. Little One got taller and had to bend down to shower me. That summer they started playing a ball game. My pot got a large crack in it from a massive white and black ball kicked into me, toppling me over. Little One was upset and Big One came out to help them. They moved me to a bigger pot. This one, green and plastic, but I still miss the colourful one.

Winter came again. Little One grew some more.

I grew taller, tall enough to reach the window. Tall enough to peak into the kitchen. I could watch them eat at the table, play on the beige indoor grass, write in books and stir soup. I did this when Little One did not come outside. I did this all winter, watching over them, and I was no longer alone.

Then summer came and I was so excited. Little One left the house more; played outside with other little ones. Little One was a lot bigger and started going out without Big One. Then Little One would go from outside to inside the house without showering me.

I got thirsty and my leafy fingers became dry. I lost some leaves; so did a lot of plants in the garden. I had watched them go yellow and fall in the time between summer and winter; now I joined them. But it felt different.

Big One came out while Little One was away. They noticed my dry leaves and parched face and brought me some water. But Little One didn't shower me anymore.

I grew taller and Little One grew taller. Big One got ever so slightly shorter. I would watch Little One go off every morning through every season, determination on their face to get wherever they were going as fast as possible. Big One was slower and started sitting with me in the summer, just looking out, watching the bees and the garden. I liked the company.

I watched the frost cling to me and everything I could see. It stayed for a long time, obscuring my view with crystals. I watched them melt in the heat later. Giving new sight. Puddles disappeared into the soil. I watched this cycle continue, over and over and over again. I grew leaves that changed colours and fell, and then grew some more. Little One got taller than Big One and spent more time away from the house. Away from me. Big One spent more time at the house and continued to sit in the garden.

Little One left and didn't come back until the winter. Big One didn't seem concerned. After a few weeks, I wasn't concerned either. I grew to trust that Little One didn't need me, but perhaps Big One did.

**P.K. BROOKES** is a queer writer and tabletop role-playing game enthusiast who loves all things weird, peculiar and horrifying. They are chronically ill and periodically funny, trying to find some light in the darkness. When not writing they talk about storytelling and gaming on Twitch. Find more at pkbrookes.com.

# The Spare Key

## Susan Goedecke

He's locked her out, again! She blinks rapidly; she will not cry. Lowering her shopping bags onto the verandah, she untangles her fingers from the skinny plastic handles that dig into her flesh. She swipes her eyes with the back of her hand, then straightens up, squares her shoulders, and breathes deeply, in and out. At the same time, she opens and shuts her hands, wiggling her fingers, feeling the familiar ache as the blood slowly seeps all the way down to her fingertips.

Cupping her hands against the glass, she peers in through the lounge room window. Barry's flat out on the recliner, head back, mouth open, the morning paper trapped under his pudgy fingers. A range of emotions play across her face as she stares at the comatose lump. Even in sleep she can see no trace of the man she fell in love with. Resigned, she lowers herself onto the front step. Experience has taught her not to disturb him. He'll let her in when he's ready.

She wonders what she's done to set him off this time. It's always her fault. That's what he says. He doesn't like having to lock her out. He's told her that often enough too. But what is he to do? He's a reasonable man, but every man has his limits. She's been living with his limits for nearly forty years.

It's warm in the sun.

A voice jolts her awake. 'Forget your key again, love?'

It's Tom from over the road, making his daily pilgrimage around the block.

'Barry should be back any minute now,' she calls out.

Tom nods, 'Good-o,' and continues on, two steps at a time behind his walking frame. She listens to his rhythm, a shuffle followed by the rasp of metal on concrete, until she can't hear it anymore.

A glance at her watch tells her she's been outside for a couple of hours. This is longer than usual, except for that time when he locked her in the shed overnight. But she doesn't like to dwell on that; it was only the once.

She stands up and stamps her feet to get the blood moving, then rests her ear against the door. Not a sound. She tests the handle. It doesn't budge. Turning towards the window, she puts her face lightly against the glass. Fear punches her in the stomach. The recliner is upright and empty; the newspaper is on the floor, pages scattered untidily on the carpet.

Barry is a fastidious man, addicted to routine. Every day after breakfast he reads the paper in his recliner. When he's finished, he writes his initials on the top right-hand corner of the front page, folds it neatly in half and puts it in her basket on the bench. Only then is she allowed to read it.

She remembers the piece of fish she cooked him for breakfast. It was only just past its use-by date. Thoroughly frightened now, she stumbles over to the fence and kneels in front of her camellia bush. Plunging her hands into the soft dirt, she wriggles her fingers until she feels plastic. She glances quickly over her shoulder before pulling a tiny ziplock bag from the soil. It contains a precious front door key. Barry doesn't know about this one. He holds all the keys to the house, says she doesn't need one now that he's retired.

Her hand is shaking so much she drops the key before she can get it into the lock. The ping as it hits the verandah paralyses her. Her breath shoots out in tiny bursts, but no sound comes from the other side of the door. Carefully, she picks it up and, using two hands, jams it into the lock. The front door swings open. There's a rush of air and she hears the back door slam.

She freezes, her legs lead weights anchoring her to the step. But the only sound is the relentless ticking of the clock on the wall in the hall. Silently, she slips through to the kitchen and looks out into the backyard. The clothes basket is lying on its side on the lawn, clumps of washing scattered on the ground. Like a sleepwalker, she wedges the back door open and steps outside.

She sees him immediately: flat on his back, on the concrete, underneath the clothesline. She creeps closer, stares at him curiously. His cheeks, usually a ruddy mottle of broken veins, are drained of colour. His mouth is crooked and his left eye is shut. It's like someone's dragged a hand down one side of his face and pulled it out of shape. The middle finger on his right hand wobbles when she says his name.

She watches him while she gathers the wet washing and gives each piece a good shake before pegging it on the line. He doesn't move, doesn't utter a sound, not even when she only uses one peg on his undies. She smiles to herself, picks up the empty basket and goes inside. There are groceries to put away and the lounge room needs straightening.

From time to time, she glances out at the clothesline. The clothes are drying nicely in the sun and Barry's right where she left him. She hums as she locks the back door and puts the kettle on. Armed with a steaming mug of tea and a packet of Tim Tams, she settles herself on the couch in front of the telly.

She opens her eyes as the evening news is starting, listens to the headlines, then remembers the washing ... and Barry.

Trembling, she picks up the clothes basket and carries it in front of her like a shield, out to the line. He hasn't moved. She says his name. His fingers are still. She pokes him with the toe of her slipper: solid as a fence post.

Carefully, she puts the clothes basket down next to Barry and walks inside. Squaring her shoulders, she takes a deep breath and picks up the phone.

**SUSAN GOEDECKE** is an emerging writer and enthusiastic people-watcher. She enjoys writing short fiction that makes you squirm. She is currently writing her first novel, a middle-grade adventure set in an abandoned defence site near her home.

# Miso Baptism

Clementine Larkins

Clumsy grabbing over the grazing table
There is no way to smoothly spread pâté onto thin wafer plates
No way to hide quince crumbs on hot tablecloth
Sun spotlights our inability to be as clean as we wish but broken
bread is a welcome rest for eyes

                        The crumbs don't stop there—
Inside it's the 2/3/4 couches that house smaller versions of
ourselves, feasting on moulding apple slices

            feasting on stray cashews between couch cushions
Then it is raining.
Olive dip containers fill quick for our black cat and we climb
into our home
In an attempt to be civilised we sit across from each other
Surrounded by your furniture and wine bottles and shame;
I peek the presence of the outside world inside of your downcast
eyes
Overcrowded countertop threatens electrical fire
But outside is the ocean, and the lake, and every raindrop with
its tiny halo

        They will find me drowned on our burnt grey carpet.
        They will find you choking on our burnt grey carpet.

But for now we eat.

We eat:

lamb shoulder slow-cooked in red wine jus
wet blush mango chicken
pork rillettes
bouillabaisse
steamed mussels.
Two days previous we slept in the car to avoid our landlord's reaching hand
(But I'm sure the confit on your chin is delicious)
The bloodied tea towels are not surprising nor unwelcome, unlike the bedpan beside your sleeping self
What sick satisfaction. My soft person houses violent actions.

I dreamed of yolks buried in salty backyard dirt

(underneath the quince tree)

The crossroad ocean rising and swallowing us all—
Swallowing all the furniture and all the bottles and all the empty pastry tins so that once the flood rolled away we'd have nothing / Be nothing but freshly purged from the salty broth / Ready to start again together, newly connected through our shared experience of which neither of us were the perpetrator / Where once the walls were wet and swollen from our miso baptism / We could sit in the remnants of our home and begin again / No longer a soft machine in the presence of your love / No longer forcing speech / A quiet understanding forged through tiredness

What a misremembered memory.

There is nothing there anymore

There is nothing
there for me
anymore.

**CLEMENTINE LARKINS** is an emerging writer and editor. They are currently working on a multidisciplinary art piece about food and consumption. You can see what they're up to on Instagram @cl3mgram.

# The Outdoor Wedding

## Joseph Sibbick

The grooms' wedding decorations were excessive, gaudy, elaborate – I was delighted. Their love was genuine, earnest and boring. Their tacky embellishments were a thrilling contrast.

Flowers of every colour were strewn over every surface, including the seats. An old lady took her cane, flicked the flowers off a chair and plopped herself down. Mother of Groom One gasped. The old lady huffed. 'I don't like the look of this. It won't end well.'

The assembled guests communicated non-verbally: *this old lady is homophobic!* We shared a collective eye roll. No gays would be dancing with her at the reception.

Old Lady's rebellion did not begin a revolution of flower flicking. Everyone else stood while the grooms walked down the aisle. Having flowers on the chairs was ridiculous, but I was relieved to stand; my pants were too tight.

It was a perfect day for an outdoor wedding. The sky was blue, but it was not too hot for complicated wedding outfits. Old Lady's ensemble was the strangest: mismatched patterns in bold colours, topped by an enormous hat, accessorised with a huge bag.

The grooms' vows were authentic, personal, emotional – it was tedious. While the grooms recounted every minute of their perfect lives together, I took in the surroundings. There were new flowers everywhere – had these flowers grown *during* the ceremony?

Old Lady huffed again as she brushed a pile of peonies off her lap. 'Does anyone have an axe?' she asked at an unsuitable volume.

Mother of Groom One pursed her rosy lips and told Old Lady that she needed to be quiet for the rest of the ceremony.

Old Lady paid no attention and continued muttering to herself as she fished around in her huge bag. She pulled out a small fire extinguisher and tossed it on the ground in frustration.

The grooms had not noticed Old Lady. They completed their promises of love and signed the papers. The flower situation had escalated to the point where the ceremonial arch began to bend under the weight of new growth. I glanced at my watch to find a vine wrapping itself around my arm.

Old Lady took large secateurs from her bag, using them to snip the vines that had grown around her feet. Passers-by at the park stared at the spectacle of flowers that went from bud to full bloom in a matter of moments. Attendees sneezed and wheezed as giant blossoms released puffs of irritating pollen. I had thought that Mothers One and Two were sniffing into their tissues at the beauty of it all, but now I realised it was allergies.

The grooms gazed at each other. Each was so captivated with the other's face that neither noticed their mothers choking on pollen and falling to the grass. Neither noticed the ceremonial arch collapsing on the celebrant.

'I knew this would happen!' Old Lady yelled. She shook her head and retrieved a length of rope from under her hat.

I worked my way over to Old Lady, slapping away the monstrous hydrangea that followed me. 'Madam, what is happening?'

Old Lady cast her eyes over my outfit. 'Can you jump in those pants?'

Jumping would strain the stitching, but I nodded.

By now, every other guest was engaged in a fight to survive. The grooms walked back down the aisle together, oblivious.

Old Lady wielded her secateurs with precision, commanding those she saved to help others. She threw me the end of the rope, which I saw was a lasso. She pointed to the grooms. 'Be ready to leap!'

The grooms kissed. They levitated, giggling as their feet left the ground. As they floated higher, they each appeared to grasp that this was not a surprise illusion that the other had planned. They clutched each other in panic.

'Help us!' Groom One screamed.

Old Lady yanked at the other end of the rope to get my attention. 'Tie them down!'

By the time I reached the grooms they were high in the air, wailing in terror. I bent my knees, engaged my glutes and leapt. The stitching of my pants was stressed to its breaking point; the sound of the ripping threads intermingled with the chorus of screams around me. It was not elegant, but I managed to loop the rope around the grooms' feet. Old Lady secured the other end to the base of a statue.

Tethered, Groom Two sneered, 'Why are there *carnations* at my wedding? The colours are all wrong!'

As soon as the grooms noticed the horrors around them, the spell was broken. The flowers went limp, their pollen settled and the attack ceased. The attendees sighed with relief, straightened their outfits and prepared for photos.

The grooms remained afloat for the reception, bobbing safely under the marquee. The rest of the guests seemed to have forgotten our ordeal by the end of the first course.

After dinner, Old Lady ushered me over. 'You have to be prepared for anything at an outdoor wedding.' Without breaking eye contact, she reached into her bag and pulled out a sewing kit. 'Come dance with me after you fix your pants.'

**JOSEPH SIBBICK** is a writer and an editor. He writes surreal, queer-themed short stories where his characters face the unexpected (often involving wayward plants). His work has been published in *Visible Ink*. Joseph is also an Australian young-adult fiction enthusiast and is writing his first novel.

# The Aftermath

Sorcha Hennessy

## Day 1

James really didn't want to get out of bed. It was freezing; he was sure his car would be frosted over. He was cocooned so deeply into his sheets, doona cover and fleecy blanket that the light from outside was hidden anyway. The alarm had been a shock to him, a normalcy he didn't expect today. Part of the surprise was that he'd even fallen asleep to be awoken by the blaring 6 am alarm. He pulled the covers tighter around him, feeling the oxygen level in his small cocoon shrinking. The more he was covered, the more he could pretend he wasn't in his bedroom, and he wasn't alone.

## Day 3

James woke up on the floor, banged his head on the bedside table and swore.

'Lucy can —' He clamped his mouth shut, partially to shut up and partially to stop the wave of nausea.

He wiggled around so that he was facing away from the bed and pulled the doona cover over his head.

## Day 4

He'd remembered to turn his alarm off, but he still woke with a start, head nearly hitting the corner of his bed base. The doorbell rang over and over. A deep, shrivelled part of his brain irked at the noise. It didn't seem so bad now. He could lie through it.

'James! I am not leaving until you open this door. I will get police to smash through every window!' Robert yelled, ringing the bell again.

James wondered if Robert meant it.

'I'm not bloody joking James! I can call a mental health check!' Rob's voice was louder, like he'd pressed his face up against the doorframe.

James knew what Robert was saying, but also didn't. He was floating outside his ragged, cold body and pondering what would happen either way.

There was a pause where silence fell, and James had the jolt of feeling empty again. He pulled himself upright and blinked slowly. Standing up was a struggle, his legs like jelly, but he reached the bedroom door and walked, dreamlike, down the hallway.

'Last chance James! I'll get the police to check you're alive if I ha —'

James interrupted him by opening the door. Rob stared at him for a moment and then pulled him into a tight hug. Rob's long curly hair tickled James's nose and he sneezed into Rob's leather jacket.

'Thanks for that.' Rob pulled away, attempting a pathetic grin, and wiped off the snot. Rob let himself in, closing the door.

They wandered into the living room. James' head began to spin and he leaned against the wall, eyes twitching. *Her pillow, her picture frames, her bookcase, her favourite book.*

'Shit, okay, perhaps not here.' Rob turned to face James and dragged him back down the hall and into James' study.

James wiped his eyes slowly and methodically; tears were just leaking out at this point. His throat stuck seeing Rob here though. He craved the feeling of nothingness back under his doona, warm and dark.

'We're putting on a movie and you are sitting here through the whole thing. I'm picking something terrible, so no complaints.' Rob pulled James's desk chair and dragged the couch forward so they could watch on the PC screen.

James watched him closely. Rob's face was blotchy and red, and he was wearing his pyjama top under his leather jacket.

## Day 5

Rob had stayed over, insisting on the floor. James was staring at the ceiling. Rob being in the house was making him antsy.

Careful not to make any noise, James padded out of the study and back into the living room. In the still-dark morning light it was distinctly less overwhelming. He continued through the room and out towards the small back garden. James was slammed back into his body by the cold, and took in a deep, hoarse breath. Tucking his hands under his arms, James made his way to the small table and chairs.

James jumped back, yelping as he saw movement amongst the table legs. The creature yelped as well and bounded to the other side of the garden. James squinted at it. It was … a rabbit?

A little grey rabbit, now curled in a cautious little hunch by James' dead tomatoes.

They stared at each other. James wondered if it was curled because of the cold, like him, or if it was scared. Just in case, he squatted down and held out a hand. The rabbit continued to stare for what felt like a whole solitary, silent minute, and then it sniffed curiously.

'Oh of course.' James looked around and then picked at some of his spinach and held it in his hand, keeping it outstretched. The rabbit sniffed again. The spinach was very small, leaves the size of the rabbit's wet nose. The rabbit looked up at James and then hopped over to him.

## Day 10

'Just these thanks.' James placed a lead and harness on the counter.

'New dog?' The clerk smiled brightly, beeping through the items.

'Rabbit.'

'Oh! How cute! How old?'

'Not sure.' James handed over his card before the clerk had finished beeping through the items. The clerk faltered but recovered, not speaking to James again. Lucy would have told him off for that.

The clerk handed over the bag and James tried to pull himself back out of his head.

'Thanks so much.' He gave a weak smile to the clerk before turning to leave.

## Day 15

James was awake at six, even though his alarm wasn't set up again and he was still off work.

The air was crisp, but the sun was out and toasting his hands as he stood in the middle of the green patch along Drummond Street. The lead in his hand was taut but he knew the length of it wouldn't reach the road, so he continued to stare out at the rows of houses like his. After a few moments, Mr Rabbit bounded over to him in a deep blue harness, the lead slackening.

'Ready to go home?'

**SORCHA HENNESSY** is a part-time writer of novels and full-time marketer of books at Hardie Grant Children's Publishing. When not emailing authors, she's delving into new worlds and avoiding onion and garlic. Her work has been published in *Phantasmagoria* and *The Maggie Journal*, and she is currently working on a fantasy novel.

# The Gods Above Us

Lydia Alexandra Best


Sun.
Star, chariot.
God of life.
Burning ember of death.
Light.

Mercury.
Poison silver.
The universe's messenger.
The sun's closest friend.
Caduceus.

Venus.
Iron core.
Born from water.
The Earth's little sister.
Desire.

Moon.
Earth's satellite.
Waxing, full, waning.
Ruler of the tides.
Selene.

Earth.
Gaea's being.
The galaxy's oasis.
3753 Cruithne, 2002 AA29.
Life.

Mars.
Scarlet sand.
Water lives beneath.
His sunsets burn blue.
War.

Jupiter.
Zeus's alter.
Raging red spot.
Io, Europa, Ganymede, Callisto.
Galileo.

Saturn.
Singing rings.
Two aspect god.
The Greek rite – uncovered.
Cronus.

Uranus.
Son, husband.
On collision tilt.
The original sky god.
Hydrogen.

Neptune.
Eighth wanderer.
The trident bearer.
The great dark spot.
Salacia.

Pluto.
Kuiper belt.
The dwarfed brother.
He, the wealthy one.
Pomegranates.

**LYDIA ALEXANDRA BEST** is a freelance photographer and writer with a passion for poetry who lives on Wurundjeri land. She has been published in regional publications that have a special interest in young writers. Lydia also spends their time working as a waiter and bartender in rural Victoria. To learn more about Lydia, visit lydiaalexandrabest.wordpress.com.

# About *Prism*

*Prism* is the final project of Towards Publication, one of the capstone subjects of RMIT's Associate Degree in Professional Writing and Editing (PWE). The writers in this anthology include fiction and non-fiction authors, poets, editors, copywriters and communications specialists. They represent an emerging generation in the Australian literary landscape.

Every student published in the anthology submitted two pieces of writing for consideration. The submissions were selected, developed, edited and proofread by the students in the anthology editing stream, who took on the role of project editors for the duration of the semester.

In line with the practical, industry-based philosophy behind the Associate Degree, the editing stream students have been responsible for the creation of the anthology, from the brainstorming of the theme to the printing of the physical book. They have been lucky to benefit from the wisdom and advice of some industry experts throughout this process, including author and editor Samone Amba and communications specialist Emma Noble.

In addition to project-editing duties of selection, structural feedback, copyediting, proofreading and project management, each project editor was also part of a small team that worked on other aspects of the anthology production.

The production team – A.I. Bartolo, Emily Foundalis, Lindy Ralph and Joseph Sibbick – made sure the schedule was followed and transformed a pile of manuscripts into a physical book. They managed the production process of typesetting and printing, and worked with typesetter, Shaun Jury, and cover designer, Josh Durham, to execute the creative vision behind *Prism*.

The marketing team – Maddox Gifford and Blaise Katherine – assisted with the launch, managed social media and promoted the anthology to RMIT students and the wider literary community.

The editorial team – Cai Bardsley, Kristin Brodie, Maddox Gifford and Mitzi Swan – created the style guide, worked on the front and back matter of the book, gave input into the text design and managed all the editing queries. They quibbled over commas and puzzled over punctuation to make sure the anthology is error-free.

Thanks goes to all staff past and present in the Associate Degree who worked to make the course, and in particular the Towards Publication subject, such a highly regarded experience. Stephanie Holt, and later Lorna Hendry, were the masterminds behind the Towards Publication editing stream in its current form. The inimitable Penny Johnson wrote the introduction, managing to encapsulate the themes contained within *Prism* and give context for the reader.

Editor and PWE teacher, Louisa Syme, went above and beyond in her role as editor for the project editors' submissions. She gave structural and copyediting feedback on the manuscripts – a privilege the project editors haven't taken for granted.

*Prism* wouldn't have been possible without Michaela Skelly, the current teacher and the anthology's managing editor. She provided endless support and guidance, as well as chocolate during the crucial 3 pm slump. Thanks go to Michaela, for keeping all plates spinning and being available for queries late into the night. You turned a class full of naive, wide-eyed students into a professional book publishing team.

**PWE PROJECT EDITORS** are a Naarm/Melbourne-based team of pedantic perfectionists who spend their days bitterly but blissfully arguing about the intricacies of grammar, punctuation, and (last but certainly not least) the much-maligned Oxford comma.